The hot Greek sun was a dangerous stimulant

Dion Stephanides slowly smoothed sun cream over Valissa's skin. "I like an element of mystery," he noted. "Not much is hidden in a bikini, but a little imagination often improves on reality."

Valissa turned slightly to look up at him. "That sounds very disillusioned."

"The girl who flaunts her body on the beach isn't necessarily uninhibited in bed," he pointed out.

She felt a blush starting and turned toward the sea. He was sure they would be lovers. If she hadn't felt the same, why had she extended her holiday?

"I like it—your modesty." His voice was suddenly deep, and he pulled her face gently toward him again. "But I don't think I'll be disillusioned with you, Valissa." Then his head bent and his mouth touched hers.

ANNE WEALE

passage to paxos

Harlequin Books

TORONTO • LONDON • LOS ANGELES • AMSTERDAM
SYDNEY • HAMBURG • PARIS • STOCKHOLM • ATHENS • TOKYO

Harlequin Presents edition published May 1982
ISBN 0-373-10504-5

Original hardcover edition published in 1981
by Mills & Boon Limited

Printed in U.S.A.

CHAPTER ONE

FOR a week of the first proper holiday she had had in four strenuous years Valissa did nothing but relax. The apartment in which she was staying had a vine-shaded roof garden overlooking the harbour of the smallest of the island's three small ports. Up there, in the heat of midday, she would sit under the canopy of green leaves, watching other holidaymakers lunching on fish and Greek salad at the tables of the waterfront tavernas. For the first seven days she felt no desire to join them, preferring to cook for herself and to eat in seclusion.

Because of its water shortage and comparative inaccessibility—it was more than three hours by sea from the nearest airport at Corfu—the island had remained unspoiled by high-rise hotels and an excess of holiday villas. The islanders, too, seemed unaffected by any of the disagreeable attitudes sometimes to be found in more crowded parts of the Mediterranean.

Here on Paxos the local people were still friendly and hospitable. Every day Anna, who cleaned the apartment, would present Valissa with a bowl of the small, delicious Paxiot olives, or some new-laid eggs or ripe figs. Clearly she was concerned that Valissa might be lonely on her own. The language barrier between them prevented the Greek woman from expressing her puzzlement as to why a presentable girl should come on holiday by herself, instead of with another girl or a group of friends, but Valissa could sense her curiosity.

But even if Anna had spoken English as well as many Paxiots did, or Valissa's command of Greek had not been limited to a smattering of essential words such as *Efharisto*, meaning Thank you, and *Kalimera*, meaning Good morning, it would have been impossible to explain why the English girl was content with her solitude.

Language was not the only barrier between them. Their backgrounds were as different as if they belonged to differ-

5

ent planets. For Valissa, a lifetime spent on a tiny Greek island, however idyllic, was unthinkable. For Anna a life without a husband and children would be equally unthinkable. She would never be able to understand that, in the wide world beyond Paxos, women now had a number of choices as to which way they wanted to live and Valissa had chosen to have a career which left her neither the time nor energy for anything or anyone else.

Not that she had set out to be a dedicated careerist. At eighteen she had been an art student in love with a fellow student whose brilliance had far outshone her own modest talent. She had thought then that marriage was her métier.

But Nick had been killed in a car crash and now, looking back, she could not be sure whether it was grief which had forged her present ambitions, or whether they had always been there, lying dormant, submerged beneath her youthful romanticism.

By the end of a week of judicious sunbathing, her skin had become a light golden brown, and she was in a mood to venture farther afield instead of never leaving the village except to bathe in the clear green water of the pebbly cove five minutes' stroll away.

Her first expedition was to Gaios, the largest town, where she bought herself a pair of green plastic sea-shoes to protect her slim feet from the pebbles, and an inexpensive silver ring in the form of a leaping dolphin.

She spent the whole day at Gaios, having supper in a side-street taverna where a number of Greek and foreign men eyed her with interest, and an Englishman tried to make friends. But Valissa was not in the market for a lighthearted holiday romance. In the tactful manner with which she had learned to deal with difficult clients, she turned down his invitation to spend the next day in his company. He did persuade her to have coffee and brandy with him at one of the several open-air cafés in the *platia*, but he could not coax her to linger and return to her village by taxi instead of by the nine-thirty bus.

The next day she rented a boat with an outboard motor. Equipped with a simple picnic of bread, wine and the white sheep's milk cheese called *feta*, she set out to explore the island's eastern coastline. The west coast, with its towering cliffs and caves, could only be cruised in a caique with a Paxiot fisherman in charge as it could be a dangerous place for the inexperienced.

It happened that Valissa had spent much of the previous night engrossed in one of the books which had formed the bulk of her luggage. In consequence, by mid-afternoon the sun and the wine conspired to make her unusually drowsy.

When she woke from her nap she saw that a fresh breeze had arisen. Out at sea, between Paxos and mainland Greece, the ocean was flecked with white horses.

She had read in her guide-book about the sudden Wagnerian thunderstorms which occurred in the month of September; and the day before, in Gaios, she had chatted to another holidaymaker whose flight had been delayed at Brindisi because of a violent downpour which had flooded the runway at Corfu for several hours.

However, being only about twenty minutes' run from the sheltered harbour of her village, she saw no reason to be alarmed by the change in the weather while she was sleeping. Briskly but calmly she re-packed her belongings in her beach bag, and waded into the thigh-deep water where the boat was anchored.

Half an hour later, instead of being safely ashore at Loggos, she was still out at sea with a motor which had suddenly died on her, and no other craft in sight from which she might hope for a tow.

There was nothing for it but to row. As her previous experience of rowing had been on the calm surface of the Serpentine in central London, the prospect of rowing at least a mile in an increasingly choppy sea with black clouds blowing up from the north-west did cause her some apprehension.

The boat had no metal rowlocks to hold the oars in position. They had to be attached to pegs by means of double loops of twine, a procedure which cost her the tips of two fingernails.

Ordinarily the damage would have made her mutter an unladylike curse, but in present circumstances broken nails seemed a triviality. She was beginning to feel she

might be lucky to save her skin. For by now, with the
oars in place, it was apparent that there was no possibility of
her rowing back to Loggos. With both wind and current
against her, she would never make it.

There was no choice but to row in the opposite direction, south towards Gaios. Knowing that from end to end
Paxos was six miles long, she estimated her present distance from Gaios as at least two miles, and with the storm
approaching much faster than she could row . . .

Closing her mind to the panic-making visions conjured
by her imagination, Valissa exerted the self-discipline
which long ago, combined with her adoration for Nick,
had enabled her to shed the teenage podge which had
been disguising the underlying slenderness of her figure.

Determined not to lose her head, she peered in the
locker to see what equipment there might be to help her
to weather this unexpected test of her mettle.

The first thing she saw was a fluorescent orange life-
jacket which at once made her feel less at risk. Although
she was a good swimmer, making all-year-round use of an
indoor pool not far from her flat in London, she felt much
safer once she was wearing the buoyancy aid.

Apart from several similar jackets, a coil of nylon rope
and a spare jerrycan for petrol, the locker contained no
other emergency equipment. No baler. No rocket or hand
flares. Watching the dark sky astern, she started to row.

By the time the first slow drops of rain began to fall, her
hands—unused to any manual work other than the light-
est domestic chores—were already beginning to feel sore.
As the storm caught up with her, the wind seemed to
come from every direction. The waves slapped this way
and that, buffeting the dinghy with a force which made
rowing even more difficult.

Soon the heavens opened, and within seconds she was
drenched, her long reddish-brown hair reduced to rats'-
tails, her tee-shirt plastered to her body.

Half blinded by the torrential deluge, she gritted her
teeth and heaved on the oars with all her strength, hauling
the blades through the turbulent water until her shoulders
and back ached with the effort.

The sea, so blue and calm when she had set out that

morning, was now as inky dark as the sky above it. For perhaps fifteen minutes—although it seemed more like an hour—the rain beat down on her until the bottom boards were awash. Then, quite suddenly, and to her infinite relief, the downpour slackened and she was able to see that now, astern, the sky was brightening a little. Evidently this storm was as localised as the one which, unbeknown to anyone on nearby Paxos, had put Corfu airport out of action.

By now, in spite of the physical exertion of rowing, she was starting to feel cold and devitalised. Painful blisters on both palms made each pull an effort of will and, from what she could see of the rocky coastline through the lighter but continuing rain, she was making very little headway.

I should have rowed back to the cove when the engine failed, left the boat there and walked back to the village, she thought, regretting her ill-judged decision to head for Gaios.

At first when she heard the approaching drone of a motor, she didn't recognise it for what it was because it seemed so unlikely that anyone else would be at sea in present conditions. No doubt all the other visitors to the island had long since returned to their holiday houses or to their favourite taverna where the locals would also be congregated. Only a person on her own would have failed to notice the signs of bad weather as she had.

The drone continued ... grew louder. Valissa rested the oars and looked over her left shoulder, hardly able to believe she was really seeing another boat, and that it was heading straight towards her.

It was not an old clinker-built inshore fishing boat such as the one she had hired, but a substantial rubber dinghy with, by the sound of it, a much larger and more reliable engine. There was only one person in it; a curly-haired, darkly tanned Greek whose wet shirt revealed broad shoulders and powerful arms.

'What you doing out here on your own?' he yelled, in English, as he came within shouting distance.

'My outboard's broken down,' she called back.

He didn't ask any more questions but set about taking

her in tow with an efficiency which suggested that she
wasn't the first lunatic tourist he had rescued from a similar predicament.

Valissa was so relieved at not having to row any farther
that she didn't care where he was taking her. It was only
now, safely under the wing of someone who knew how to
cope with situations of this sort, that she realised how
terrified she had been deep down inside her.

She began to shiver, partly with cold and partly with
the aftermath of tension. Her teeth were chattering by the
time they reached a sheltered bay where the Greek cut
his engine and let the boat's momentum bring her alongside a small jetty built out from the rocks and fitted with
several stout iron rings.

'Don't move. Sit still,' was his somewhat brusque command before, sure-footed as the island sheep which she
had seen scrambling up the drystone retaining walls of
the hillside olive groves, he sprang lightly ashore to moor
his craft with the deftly-tied knot of the experienced
seaman.

On his feet, he was taller than she had expected him to
be. Few of the Greeks she had encountered were of more
than medium height, and most of the old men were an
inch or two smaller than she was. However, this particular
Greek was not far short of six foot, and the broad shoulders
and muscular upper torso which suggested that he might
earn his living by hauling in nets or wielding a pick-axe
was not matched by short sturdy legs. His tight rain-
soaked jeans moulded long legs and narrow hips.

'Now you may move.'

Drawing the bows of the hired boat close to the concrete
landing stage, he held out his other hand to help her
ashore.

What surprised her about his grip was not its strength
but its warmth. Whereas she felt chilled to the bone, his
fingers were as warm as if the sun were still shining.

Having landed beside him without mishap she then
found that the jetty, instead of feeling blessedly stable,
seemed to be pitching and tossing as the boat had a short
time earlier.

There being nothing else to grab at, Valissa clutched at

the Greek to steady herself while she recovered her land legs. The next instant she was in his arms, not vertically but horizontally. As easily as if she were a skinny thirteen-year-old instead of a slim but not featherweight twenty-three, he scooped her up, close to his chest, and before she could recover from her surprise, he was carrying her over the rocks between the jetty and the beach.

At the back of the beach a rough track led upwards through dense prickly scrub.

'Oh please . . . you can't carry me uphill. I'm all right now. I'll walk,' she protested, when he failed to set her on her feet.

The Greek ignored her objection, and indeed the steep slope of the path seemed to make her no more of a burden than she had been before. He was obviously superbly fit to an extent seldom achieved by the men of her own milieu even though most of them played squash regularly, or worked out in gymnasiums to combat the ill effects of their sedentary jobs.

She did not protest a second time. She had offered to walk out of consideration for her rescuer, but if carrying her really was no hardship to him she was happy to stay where she was. His body was as warm as his hand. It was like leaning against a radiator, except that his chest was more comfortable.

'We are coming to the steepest place. Put your arm round my neck,' he ordered.

Valissa obeyed, encircling his neck with her left arm and linking her fingers on a level with his collarbone.

Once or twice, in the long ago of her carefree student days, Nick had swept her off her feet, whirling her round before kissing her. Since then no other man had touched her, or at least not for more than the few seconds it had taken to extricate herself from an unwelcome embrace. None of the men who had tried to begin to make love to her could claim that she had encouraged them. Probably it had been her total lack of interest in men as men which had spurred a few of them to attempt to break through her detachment.

For more than a year after Nick's death she had been too shattered, too heartbroken to feel anything except a despairing longing to have his arms round her once more, and the bitter ache of regret that they had never been lovers in the fullest sense.

Later, when the agony of grief began to dull a little, she was too immersed in her work to have time for many social activities. In any case, most of the men she met were either other women's husbands or not heterosexual.

She accepted invitations to dinner parties because they might bring useful contacts; but dinners à *deux* she turned down with some polite excuse, preferring to spend the time working. And for a girl who was prepared to devote all her time and energy to her job, it was, she discovered, very easy to climb the chosen ladder.

Edward Cornford, Valissa's dearly loved grandfather, now in his eighty-third year, was fond of quoting Thomas Edison's aphorism—*Genius is one per cent inspiration and ninety-nine per cent perspiration.*

Valissa had no pretensions to genius, although she believed that the world might have lost one in Nick. Applied to herself, she amended the maxim to *Success is one per cent luck and ninety-nine per cent concentration.*

Thus, having for four years abstained from any emotional involvement by sublimating her instincts in a passionate absorption in her work, it was disconcerting to find that now, in the arms of a man who was merely being a good Samaritan, those long-repressed feelings were reviving.

'Is there a village at the top?' she asked, trying to ignore the fact that, suddenly, she was enjoying being in his strong arms for another reason than that she was weary from rowing.

'No, only my grandmother's cottage where you can put on dry clothes and rest till this bad weather passes. Later I'll look at your motor and see if I can get it going.'

This idiomatic reply, spoken with not even the slightest of Greek accents, made her realise she had been mistaken in thinking he might not speak much English. Clearly he spoke it very well, and it had been a trick of the wind which had made his first shouted question sound ungrammatical.

'Where were you going when you spotted me?' she asked.

'Nowhere. I was at the cottage, watching the storm, when I saw your boat come past the headland. In weather like this, it would have been wiser to head for shore as soon as your motor failed.'

'I know. I realised I'd made the wrong decision. Lucky for me you saw me—I couldn't have gone on much longer. My palms feel on fire,' she admitted.

'Blistered them, have you?'

'Yes. I'm not used to rowing.'

'So I noticed,' was his somewhat caustic comment. A moment later he softened it by adding, 'But at least you are not in tears or hysterics as many young girls would be after a similar experience. Why were you alone in the boat? Had a tiff with your boy-friend and left him to hike home?' He sounded as if the idea amused him.

'I'm not here with a boy-friend . . . or any friends. I came to Paxos for two weeks of total peace and quiet.'

The path had begun to level out, revealing, through the slackening rain, a small whitewashed cottage with an uneven roof of old clay tiles, and two windows with shutters on either side of the front door. This was reached by a short flight of steps flanked by two enormous ribbed pots of the kind used for water storage on an island where, until fairly recently, all water had come from the sky, there being no springs to supply it.

Now, so Valissa had been told, the people of Gaios had water piped from a borehole. But elsewhere on Paxos both islanders and tourists were dependent on reserves of rain-water held in underground cisterns or, when these were exhausted, on the services of a water truck.

Because of the acute water shortage, and the generally inefficient plumbing, the island, for all its beauty, was not a place which many of her clients—accustomed to the highest level of luxury—would have found an enjoyable resort. But for Valissa herself, although she was used to every convenience, the long days of brilliant sunshine and the warmth of the pale jade green water more than compensated for the primitive sanitation. Especially after a particularly sunless summer in England.

At the foot of the steps, between the water jars which now served as pots for geraniums, the Greek set her lightly on her feet but kept his right arm round her waist to help her mount the steps.

The door was not locked. He pushed it open and, to her surprise, reached inside to switch on a light. She would have supposed that so isolated a dwelling would be lit by oil lamps or candles.

They entered the house, stepping directly into a kitchen which seemed to be also the living-room. An old-fashioned wood-burning cooking stove was the dominant feature, but evidently it was no longer used as a modern electric cooker had been installed alongside it.

However, for the moment Valissa was more interested in her companion than in the interior arrangements of his grandmother's cottage. Until now the rain and the dark clouds still scudding overhead had made it difficult to see his face in detail, although a few discreet glances while he was carrying her uphill had given her an impression of a strongly marked profile, the big nose curved like a scimitar and the chin aggressively square.

'The towels are kept in my grandparents' room. You can dry yourself there,' he said, opening the door of the adjoining room which also had electric light.

While he went to a cupboard in one corner, Valissa hesitated on the threshold, looking at the high double bed covered with an immaculate white counterpane.

'Won't they mind a stranger invading their bedroom?' she asked doubtfully.

'They're no longer here,' he replied, still with his back to her. 'My grandfather died when I was a small boy, and my grandmother during the summer. But if they were here, they would only be concerned for your comfort. The older generation of country people are always glad to meet strangers and make them welcome.'

With a stack of towels over his arm, he closed the cupboard door and turned towards her. For the first time she saw him full face, and in the revealing glare of the unshaded light bulb hanging from the centre of the ceiling.

Not with any personal admiration, but purely from an artistic point of view, she had noticed a number of Greeks whose faces had pleased her eye. But none, she discovered, staring at him, to compare with the wet, dark-skinned face of her rescuer.

He was not as young as she had thought him. The muscular hardness of his body above and below his leather belt had misled her into thinking him her own age. Now she could see he was older; thirty, perhaps thirty-five. Nor was he, strictly speaking, handsome. In fact not handsome at all, and yet most compellingly attractive with those strange-coloured golden-grey eyes, and that wide, sensual, humorous mouth.

Having tossed several towels on the bed, he said, 'There are no women's clothes I can give you. You will have to wear some of mine. I'll bring them to you in a few minutes. The first thing to do is to strip off and dry yourself thoroughly.'

With which advice he left the room.

One of the towels he had left her was large enough for her to wrap it round herself sarong-fashion. This done, she used a smaller towel to turban her hair and stop it dripping. With the third towel she dried her chilled feet. The damage to her hands made it difficult to do this with sufficient friction to make her feet warm again.

The Greek was much quicker than she was. She had just finished drying her feet and was about to unwrap the turban when he tapped on the door. Barely giving her time to call 'Come in', he reappeared in a dry pair of jeans but with nothing on the upper half of his body.

Naked, his physique was even more impressive than when seen through a rain-drenched shirt. Compared with the mahogany sheen of his chest and shoulders, Valissa's skin still seemed quite pale.

'If your hands are painful, you had better let me rub your hair dry,' he said. 'Just how bad are your blisters? Show them to me.'

Obediently she turned her hands palms upward for his inspection. Usually she wore several rings, including the one given to her by Nick on the day he had asked her to marry him.

They had both been born under Gemini, and although neither of them had taken astrology too seriously, the ring he had chosen had been a modern representation of the Heavenly Twins, designed and made by a friend of his who was training to become a silversmith.

Some of her girl friends had thought it a strange ring to mark an engagement. But Valissa, like Nick, was not attracted by precious stones except of the sort that were far beyond his limited budget. She had found it less painful to go on wearing what most people took for a dress ring.

At the moment, however, her fingers were bare of ornaments as she wore them only in the evening. She didn't like jewellery at the beach and, for the same reason, had changed her nail varnish from the dark, rich colours she wore in London to a pale pearlised shade which she thought more appropriate in Paxos.

The man she worked for insisted that taste be applied to every aspect of life no matter how trifling, and Valissa agreed with his precept. She would no more have signed her name with the characterless line of a blue ballpoint than she would have dropped litter in the street.

Now her keen sense of detail was focussed on the man beside her, noting that his hands also were ringless. He wore neither the broad gold band of the Greek married man, nor any of the ornate rings for men she had seen in the shops in Gaios.

His ears were unpierced, his strong brown throat bare of necklets. She found herself thinking that no man who looked like Zeus on a visit to earth needed any of those adornments. He had only to look as he did—tall and fit and splendidly virile—to catch and hold female glances far more surely than the man with the flashy medallion or the status-symbol wrist-watch.

'Hm . . . I don't think they'll take long to heal. Some antiseptic powder and a dry dressing is probably the best treatment for them,' he said. 'Sit down on the bed and I'll give your hair a good rub.'

His idea of a good rub was the vigorous towelling which, when Valissa was a little girl, her grandmother had administered to her dogs when they came back wet after one of their owner's energetic country walks. By the time he had finished, she was flushed, wildly tousled and slightly breathless.

'Thank you. Oh dear . . . how stupid of me! I left my beach bag in the boat.'

'I'm not going to offer to fetch it because it's perfectly safe where it is, and it must have been wet through already. If it's a comb you want you can use mine.'

He went away and came back with an immaculately clean tortoiseshell comb. His nails, too, were scrupulously clean, as she had already noticed, and neither broken nor stained with nicotine like the nails of most fishermen and labourers.

Perhaps he was one of the island's several taxi-drivers, or maybe a waiter who had perfected his English by chatting up susceptible female tourists.

'While you're combing your hair and getting dressed, I'll go and warm up some soup. I haven't eaten since this morning, and a bowl of hot soup won't do you any harm after that soaking,' he told her.

Left alone, Valissa examined the clothes he had provided for her. They were a pair of white linen shorts and a shirt of dark coral cotton. He had also found an elasticated belt to slot through the loops on the shorts and adapt the waistband to her measurements.

Having dressed, she dealt with her hair, which was not as tangled as she had feared. There was no mirror in the bedroom in which she could look at herself before going through to the other room. Not that her lack of make-up bothered her. She had worn none since her first day on Paxos, nor had she put up her hair as she did every morning in London.

Here, she wore it in a thick, glossy plait by day, and loose on her shoulders after dark. Luckily her lashes and eyebrows were several shades darker than her hair, so her eyes did not lack definition when she left off shadow and mascara.

Her large deep blue eyes, her one beauty, were an inheritance from her mother, the lovely Alethea Makepeace whose name was almost forgotten now, but who had been one of the first British actresses to become famous in a long-running television series. She and Valissa's father had died in an air disaster when their daughter was only a year old, but fortunately James Cornford's parents had been happy to take charge of their grandchild.

At that time, although in their sixties, they had both
been extremely active. It was not until her late teens that
Valissa had become aware that in certain ways she was
different from girls whose parents had reared them.

Most parents could come to terms with the change in
morals since their young days. Some might not like the
new standards, and some might actively oppose them. But
upsetting one's parents, she felt, was not nearly as bad as
distressing one's darling old grandparents, now in their
seventies and in declining health.

For this reason, while many of her friends were experi-
menting with sex, Valissa had remained on the sidelines,
held back from indulging her own eager curiosity by an
instinctive feeling that it would be wiser to wait for her
true love to materialise, and also by the knowledge that
Granny and Grandpa would be most bitterly hurt if they
ever found out that *she* was taking the Pill.

Strangely, it was his suspicion that she was still a virgin
which had attracted Nick to her. He had been a good-
looking young man, accustomed to easy conquests and
somewhat bored with them. Valissa's inexperience had
intrigued him. Later, loving her, and wanting very much
to make love to her, he had found himself restrained by
several factors.

In the first place he had begun to share her affection
and respect for her grandparents. The two kind old people
lived by standards which had never been exemplified in
his own family. He knew they trusted him not to go far
beyond the bounds of what had been allowable between
an engaged couple in their own youth.

Equally, he had been restrained by the fact that, it
being winter, there was nowhere for them to make love
except in a hurried, hole-and-corner fashion, and he
hadn't wanted Valissa's initiation to be spoiled by the
wrong surroundings.

Had they fallen in love in the spring, the privacy and
beauty offered by the summer countryside might have
proved too great a temptation, for Valissa had been as
impatient to discover the pleasures of love as he had been
to teach her.

But before the summer he was dead, and since then her

heart and her body had remained untouched. At twenty-three, she was still a virgin, and likely to remain one—or so she would have said yesterday, had she thought about it.

Yet now, all at once, because a tall, well-built stranger had carried her in his arms, she was keyed up in a way she had almost forgotten.

As she opened the door and saw him standing by the cooker, she found herself thinking: What would it be like to be kissed by him? What would it be like in bed with him?

The latter thought shocked and dismayed her. What had come over her that she could contemplate making love with a man she had never set eyes on until half an hour ago?

'It's almost ready. Sit down,' he said.

She saw that he had spread a cloth on the table, and laid it with spoons and knives, paper napkins and two cheap tumblers. There was also a loaf of bread, a bottle of wine and a dish of black olives.

'This is a fish soup made for me by the woman who does my washing and cleans up now that I'm on my own here,' he said, setting a bowl of it before her.

'It looks delicious,' she said.

And it did; a soup quite unlike the tasteless stuff, made from a packet of powder and boiling water, which so often passed for soup in England. As well as having substantial chunks of fish in it, this soup was thick with pieces of potato, haricot beans, onions, bits of green beans and green pepper, all simmered together into a rich, filling broth well-seasoned with pepper and garlic.

The Greek cut some thick slices of bread and offered one to her on the point of the bread knife.

'I have only red wine in the house. Will you have some?' he asked.

'Thank you ... just half a glass,' she added, the tumblers being large ones.

For some minutes they ate in silence, Valissa with her bare feet tucked on the rung of her chair to keep them off the flagstoned floor. They were still cold, but she didn't like to ask him if he had any socks she could borrow until he had finished his meal. Fortunately her blistered palms did not make it difficult to eat and drink. It was only activities which involved the flats of her hands which were painful.

'What's your name, and where are you staying?' he enquired presently.

'Valissa Cornford, and I'm staying at Loggos. What's your name?'

He was in the act of lifting his spoon to his lips, and he swallowed the mouthful of soup before he said, 'Dion.'

'Short for Dionysios?'

'Yes.'

'Who was the son of Zeus and Samele, a princess of Thebes, who had a miscarriage and died. But the baby was sewn up in his father's thigh and delivered three months later, which is why he was called twice-born and became immortal. Is that right?'

He shrugged, as if Greek mythology was of little interest to him. 'Probably. I know he was supposed to have discovered how to make wine. *Ya sas!*' He raised his glass to her.

Valissa echoed the toast, and sampled the wine, conscious that Dion was continuing to watch her after she had looked away.

'It's too late in the year for a schoolmistress to be on holiday. You're a nurse, perhaps?' he suggested.

She shook her head. 'You're miles out. I'm an interior designer.' In case the term might mean nothing to him, she added, 'I help people to decorate and furnish their houses ... rich people who haven't the time or the inclination or the taste to do it themselves. I'm not a designer in my own right yet. At the moment I work for a famous designer who has to have a team of assistants or he'd never be able to cope with all his commissions.'

'So the customers pay a lot of money, thinking they're buying his ideas, but what they're really getting is your ideas, although he's the one who takes the big rake-off; is that how it works?' he asked, with a sardonic half-smile.

Oh, dear, was he going to turn out to be a rabid Red? One of those boring militants who turned every conversation into a political harangue. Up the proletariat; down with the bloated capitalists.

'No, it's not like that at all,' she said firmly. 'Usually every client has a personal consultation with Eliot to begin with, and he lays down the broad outlines. We just deal with the details and the donkey-work—although that's a bad way to describe it because it's enormously interesting. What do you do for a living?'

'In my time I've done many things. You could call me a jack-of-all-trades. At present, like you, I'm on holiday. Have some more soup?'

'No, thank you. I thoroughly enjoyed it, but I couldn't manage another helping. Where did you learn your remarkable English? I speak a little French, but I've no idea what their word is for a jack-of-all-trades. You don't even have an accent. Anyone overhearing you would think it was an Englishman speaking.'

'The Greeks are like the Dutch. If they want to do business with foreigners they have to be linguists because so few people speak their language. I've had the advantage of living in England. But I think I do have a slight accent if you listen closely. I must make more effort to get rid of it.'

'Why try when it's such an advantage?'

He lifted an eyebrow. 'An advantage?'

'With women. A foreign accent has been knocking women for six since Maurice Chevalier was young. If I were you I should cultivate it a little, not try to get rid of it,' she said.

He laughed, showing excellent teeth. Then his unusual eyes narrowed slightly and he put his elbows on the table and leaned towards her.

'Does my accent knock you for six?' he asked, deliberately accentuating the foreign intonation which before she had not even noticed.

Valissa felt her heartbeat quicken, and a trembly sensation began inside her. This time she did not look away. She could not. His gold-grey eyes held her gaze and would not let it go.

She was conscious of two things. First, that she was in the field of a physical magnetism even stronger than Nick's attraction for her. Secondly, that the man on the other side of the table might merely be flirting with her, or he might be leading up to a situation which could be even more unpleasant than her recent ordeal on the sea.

As she was fumbling for an answer, he suddenly rose from the table, making her give an involuntary nervous jerk backwards. Before she could recover from the recoil, he had moved away towards the shallow stone sink to fill a kettle from the tap. But she knew her reaction had not passed unnoticed, and when he had set the kettle on the hob, he glanced at her and said, on a faintly derisive note, 'You needn't be nervous, Miss Cornford. To employ another English expression, you have not survived the deep sea only to find yourself supping with the devil. My intentions towards you are entirely innocuous, I assure you.'

'I—I didn't think they weren't,' she stammered in embarrassment.

'I believe it crossed your mind,' he said dryly. 'Which is natural enough. This is an isolated place, and I'm a stranger. Why should you trust me?'

She could think of nothing to say to this, so she helped herself to an olive and wondered if she would see him again, once their present encounter was over.

Whatever his intentions might be, the look he had given her had suggested that the attraction she felt was not entirely one-sided. Perhaps he would seek her out at Loggos, although with only five days of her holiday left. . . .

'I'm making instant coffee tonight because not many tourists really enjoy Greek coffee,' said Dion. 'Afterwards I'll dress your hands, and then you can rest while I go down and see what can be done to get your outboard going. If the light goes before I've fixed it, I can bring it up here and work on it.'

'Wouldn't it be much simpler to run me back to Loggos in your boat, and let the man who owns it worry about the other boat?' she suggested. 'Naturally I would reimburse you for the cost of the petrol you used.'

'You must never offer money to Paxiots who try to help you out of a difficulty. It causes grave offence.'

'I'm sorry . . . I didn't mean to offend you. But I do seem to be causing you a great deal of trouble. I'm sure you must have better things to do this evening than tinker with my outboard,' she answered.

'On the contrary, tinkering with engines is something I enjoy and rarely have the chance to do. If whoever owns it doesn't service it properly, it could let you down a second time. Even in fine weather, it's a bore when an outboard conks out. And you certainly can't do any more rowing till those blisters are better.'

'No, but . . . well, if you're sure you don't mind.' She had been going to say 'Actually I only hired it for one day' but had changed her mind.

Later he produced such a well-equipped first aid kit, and dealt with her hands so competently that she wondered if he might be a doctor. But if he was, why hadn't he said so?

Maybe she was making too much of his educated English, and his acceptable table manners. He hadn't slurped his soup, and he had tilted the bowl away from himself. But was that conclusive proof that, although the grandson of peasants, he was not one himself?

What did it matter anyway? Valissa asked herself. But the truth was that although she had never thought of herself as a snob, something in her shied from the idea of engaging in a holiday idyll with a man whose background was completely different from her own simply because of his irresistible machismo.

Besides, there wasn't time for an idyll, and in any case Dion looked the sort of man who would only pursue a girl with a view to getting her into bed. And that, thought Valissa, was definitely not on in her case.

However, when he suggested that, while he went down to the jetty, she should rest on his grandparents' bed, she did not demur, as she did feel extraordinarily tired.

'Have a nap. It will do you good. I'll wake you as soon as the boat is ready,' he told her. 'Don't worry, the bed isn't damp. I've been sleeping in it myself. It's more comfortable than the single bed in the other room.'

When she had watched him striding away down the hill, she washed up the few supper things, and then turned back the spotless white coverlet and lay down on the bed where his grandmother had spent her wedding night, and borne her children, and died.

Had she loved her husband? Valissa wondered drowsily.

Or had she merely accepted him, because for a Paxiot girl of her generation there had been no option? Perhaps, if he had looked like Dion. . . .

She awoke with a sob of relief, thinking at first that the arms which held her were Nick's. He had been a part of her nightmare, and it was several minutes before she registered that the soothing masculine voice was not his but one which she recognised yet could not quite place.

Trembling, she clung to whoever it was who was holding her. Confused, still gripped by the terror of her dream, she babbled, 'Oh, please . . . do be careful. . . .'

'I always am. What's the trouble, Valissa?'

'The water's so deep . . . there are sharks here. . . .'

Then she woke up properly, knowing where she was, and in whose arms.

'Oh . . . I was dreaming . . . I'm sorry. . . .'

'No need to apologise. Anyone can have a nightmare.' He continued to hold her close to him, one arm firmly round her back, the other stroking her head.

Her breathing steadied. She gave a deep sigh and relaxed, knowing herself safe from the horrors which had seemed so real before he woke her.

'Was I shouting? I used to sometimes, when I was little.'

'You were obviously shouting in your dream, but the sounds you were making were more like whimpers. If I hadn't left the door slightly open after coming in to look at you earlier, I doubt if I'd have heard you.'

On one side the bedroom was bright with the light of an almost full moon flooding in through the small window which pierced the thick stone outer wall.

'What time is it? Is the boat ready?' she asked, pulling back to look up at him.

'Yes, but as you were sleeping very soundly it seemed a pity to wake you. Anyway, I thought it inadvisable for you to go back in the dark—even this bright dark. Had you not been in a deep sleep, I'd have taken you back under tow. As it was, I thought you might as well stay here till the morning.'

'Till the morning!' she echoed, taken aback.

'Don't worry: your failure to turn up by sundown won't have caused a panic in the village. I sent word to say you were safe, and they needn't start searching the coast for you.'

'You sent word? How?'

'By telephone—there's one in the taverna half a mile from here. I wrote out a message, and one of my neighbour's children delivered it to the man who keeps the taverna. He will have rung his brother in Loggos who will have informed the boat's owner and the woman in charge of your apartment.'

'But, Dion, I can't spend all night here!'

'Why not? Because we're alone? You needn't worry about that. It won't set the tongues wagging in Loggos, if that's what concerns you. They would have gossiped at one time, but not any more. They've been in the tourist game long enough to accept the way foreigners behave. Topless bathers, nude bathers, couples who aren't married, hippies, drunken yachtsmen—the Paxiots have seen it all by now, and they no longer bat an eyelid.'

'But you said you were using this bed . . . that the other one wasn't comfortable.'

'It won't hurt me to spend one night on it. I don't need as much sleep as most people. Four or five hours is enough for me. That's why I was still reading in the other room when you cried out. Go back to sleep now, Valissa. As soon as it's light, I'll wake you. You'll have a grandstand view of the sunrise, and be back in your own apartment in time for an early breakfast.'

'I—I don't know that I can sleep again. How long have I been asleep already?'

'About six hours. It was about seven when I left you, and now it's a little after one. But after a scare such as you had, you need extra sleep to recover.'

'Do I?'

It seemed to her that although this might have been true earlier, at this particular moment she had never been more wide awake. He still held her loosely embraced, and her hands still lay on his chest where, at first, she had clutched at his shirt. All the time they had been talking, she had been increasingly aware of the strength of his encircling arm and the solid wall of bone and muscle where her hands were resting.

Even through the bandages he had put on, she could feel the slow, steady beat of his heart against her right palm. In the silvery gloom beyond the bright beam of moonlight, his eyes were shadowed and mysterious between the jut of his brows and the high, pronounced slant of his cheekbones.

He looked like another god now—not Zeus, the supreme immortal, but his foster-brother Pan, the god of the woods and wild places.

A tremor ran through her. Her breath seemed to catch in her throat. At the same time she felt his heart change its beat, becoming stronger, more rapid. His arm tightened, drawing her to him until, through two layers of thin cotton, the softness of her breasts was lightly pressed to his hard chest.

She saw his head bend to hers, knew he was going to kiss her, and found herself powerless to stop him . . . unwilling to stop him. Even before his lips pressed gently on hers, she had closed her eyes in mute submission.

His first kiss was like the match flame which ignites the swift conflagration of a bonfire sprinkled with petrol. For a few seconds only his mouth moved lightly on hers, letting her keep her lips closed but making them quiver with the shock of an almost forgotten sensation.

Then, abruptly, the arm round her tightened, and she felt the fierce heat of desire blaze up, not only in him but also in her.

She tore her mouth free. 'No . . . no. . . .'

But it was only a token protest, for her arms had crept round his neck, and her body was not resisting him.

Dion knew it, and reclaimed her mouth, leaning over her in such a way that she was forced to sink back against the high mound of the old-fashioned bolster and pillows.

And Valissa, knowing it was madness, but at the mercy of emotions too long and unnaturally repressed, let him press kisses on her slim throat and begin to unbutton her shirt.

CHAPTER TWO

WITH only one button unfastened, he suddenly jerked up his head and muttered some Greek exclamation which sounded impatient and angry. An instant later he was sitting on the side of the bed, raking his fingers through his thick curly crop, and shaking his head as if to clear it.

'You were right. You can't stay here,' he said huskily. 'Come on, I'll take you back to Loggos.'

With which statement he rose to his feet and crossed to the door, opening it wide so that the electric light from the other room outlined his tall figure as he paused on the threshold, looking back at her.

Valissa lay where he had left her, unable to adjust to this sudden sharp drop in an emotional temperature which, seconds before, had been close to boiling point.

'Come on, Valissa,' he said sharply. 'I'm not Superman. If you go on lying there I may change my mind. Up you get, there's a good girl.'

He turned away. She saw him walk the length of the kitchen to the stone sink where he ran the tap and bent over to cup his hands under the flow and dash cold water on his face.

Still feeling dazed and bewildered, she struggled into a sitting position and swung her legs over the edge of the bed. The emerald green sandals she had bought in Gaios and had been wearing when he rescued her were still on the floor where she had taken them off before drying her feet. Although invaluable on stony beaches, they were not very comfortable to wear otherwise, which was why she had not put them on again. Now she carried them into the other room and sat down to put them on and fasten the buckles.

Dion said, 'It's cool on the sea at this time of night. You'll need a sweater. I'll get one for you.'

He walked past her and disappeared.

Her straw beach bag was on the table, not as badly the

worse for wear as she had expected. She ran a comb
through her hair and plaited it, her fingers clumsier than
usual because her hands were shaking. It was beginning
to hit her that she had made a fool of herself—worse than
a fool. What must he think of a girl who was willing to
abandon herself to a stranger?

He came back with two sweaters; one a navy blue
ribbed jersey with cotton reinforcements on the shoulders
and elbows, the type worn by Royal Navy personnel and
many civilians as well. The other sweater was grey, a softer
garment not intended for hard wear. This he held out to
her.

'Thank you.' It was an effort to meet his eyes, and she
knew a deep flush of shame was suffusing her face. 'Is . . .
is there a privy I could use before we leave?'

'There is, and it's not at the bottom of the garden. We
have an indoor lavatory, although it's not too efficient—
few Paxos loos are. In the interests of saving water, don't
flush it if you only spend a penny.' He smiled at her
suddenly. 'How's that for command of idiom?'

His smile almost made her feel better; as if what had
happened in the bedroom was not so shaming after all.

It was not as if she had led him on. It wasn't her fault
she had had a nightmare. What had followed had not
been her doing, but his. She had not invited his kiss,
except to the extent of being a girl, and letting him keep
his arms round her when it was no longer necessary.

All these arguments flashed through her mind, but they
didn't outweigh the conviction, instilled by her grandmother, that the onus for controlling an emotional situation always rested on the girl, not the man.

Considering her generation, old Mrs Cornford had been
a broadminded realist.

'You're going to be a beauty like your mother, dearest,'
she had told Valissa, who had known that it wasn't really
true but just Granny trying to boost the morale of a plump
teenager at whom, as yet, no boy had looked at twice.

'And when a girl is very lovely,' Mrs Cornford had
continued, 'a great many young men want to make love
to her. You wouldn't think so to look at me now, but I
was considered rather a pretty girl myself, so I had some

of the problems which you will have to deal with. Except
that, when I was young, men expected us to say No—
whereas nowadays, from what one hears, the reverse is
the case. However, whatever else changes, human nature
never alters very much. A young man's emotions have
always been far more inflammable than a girl's, which is
something she shouldn't forget. It's both unkind and
unfair to excite expectations which one doesn't intend to
fulfil.'

Remembering her grandmother's gentle homily,
Valissa felt a fresh wave of chagrin that it had been Dion,
not she, who had called a halt to an episode which, had it
run its course, could only have left her more deeply
ashamed and humiliated.

Neither of them spoke as they walked down the hill
path and he handed her into her boat.

In the stillness of the brilliant night—the sea was as
calm as if the storm had never happened—the starting
snarl of the motor sounded much louder than by day.
With his dinghy in tow astern, they set out on the run to
Loggos.

In spite of her profound discomfiture, Valissa could not
ignore the beauty of the Ionian seascape as she sat on the
thwart, facing forward, with Dion behind her, steering
the dinghy.

To her left lay the island clad with olives and, here and
there, the dark spire of a columnar cypress. To the north
were the two large rocks rising out of the water and
marking a weed-covered reef. To the east, the cliffs and
high mountains of the mainland were just dimly dis-
cernible in the distance.

'A sailing dinghy is better. Engines can be convenient, but on a night like this they're an intrusion,' said
Dion.

She nodded agreement without turning her head to
glance at him.

'It's a pity you've tied back your hair. It's something I
like to see—a girl's hair blowing loose in the wind.'

His tone held a faint note of mockery, as if the sight of
her primly upright back amused him in view of her wan-
tonness earlier.

Her breeze-cooled cheeks warmed at the memory of his hot lips searing her throat as he started to undo the shirt he had lent her. Why had he stopped? What scruple had made him desist in circumstances in which most men would have had no compunction in making the most of the situation?

The run back did not take long. Soon they were passing the cove which had been her bathing place the week before, and then taking a sweeping curve around the promontory behind which lay Loggos with its whitewashed, russet-roofed houses, now mostly unlighted as their occupants slept undisturbed except by the noise of roosters which, on Paxos, did not herald the dawn merely, but crowed all through the night.

Anna had laughed when Valissa indicated to her that she found the roosters rather tiresome. Probably the local people were not woken up by the outbursts of crowing, just as Valissa could sleep through the noise made by rubbish collectors who, in her part of London, did their work at five in the morning.

'When I was a small boy, this waterfront used to be lit by oil lanterns,' said Dion, as he cut the engine and let the two linked boats glide towards a space in the row of craft moored at the quay facing the mouth of the harbour.

'Stay where you are but just shift a little to one side,' he added, as they neared the space he had chosen.

Valissa did as he told her, and he rested a hand on her shoulder as he stepped lightly past her, reaching the bows in time to stop them bumping too heavily against the edge of the quay. Moments later he was ashore, the boat secured and his hand extended to help her to follow him.

'I'll see you as far as your door,' he said quietly, before she could murmur her thanks and bid him goodnight.

'Please don't bother. It's not far. Nobody's going to mug me in Loggos.'

'No, but I prefer to come with you.' He took her basket from her hand and, with his free hand, gripped her lightly but firmly by the elbow.

The apartment in which she was staying was the top

floor of a tall house built against a steeply sloping bank
between two lanes, one of which gave access to Valissa's
quarters, and the other to the lower floors. She had rented
it from a friend of her art school days who now was doing
rather well as a magazine illustrator and had bought the
whole building as a holiday home and an investment.

The flat was attractively decorated with inexpensive but
stylish Laura Ashley papers and fabrics, and Habitat
accessories. It consisted of one large room with twin beds
arranged at right angles with a lamp table in the corner
between them. During the day, piled with cushions, they
served as sofas. A very small kitchen and a shower room
completed the accommodation, which was greatly
enhanced by the dappled shade of the terrace with its roof-
top view of the village and harbour.

At the top of the steps she asked for her beach bag
which contained the large, old-fashioned key which
opened her door. As she fitted it into the lock, she said, 'If
you can wait a few minutes, I'll give you your clothes
back.'

'I don't need them now. I'll collect them the next time
I'm over here. I do my shopping in Loggos.'

'I might be out when you come.'

'Then leave them with your maid. Where does she
live?'

'In the cottage at the bottom of the steps. Yes, all right,
that's what I'll do. Well . . . goodbye, and thank you very
much for helping me and putting the boat right.'

Valissa held out her hand in a formal gesture of fare-
well.

Dion's brown fingers closed over hers, exerting a brief
but firm pressure. 'Goodnight, Valissa.'

He turned and walked the short distance back to the
steps where he lifted a hand and disappeared.

She entered the flat, locking the door behind her. Then
she put her bag on a chair and, without switching on any
lights, walked across the room to the french doors giving
on to the terrace. They were the room's only ventilation
and she left them open at all times. The striped Greek rug
inside the threshold was damp when she bent to feel it,
otherwise the storm had done no harm. The mat would

soon dry in the morning sun.

Knowing that, if he glanced up, he wouldn't be able to
see her standing in the shadow of the vine, she crossed to
the railing and waited for Dion to reappear on the waterfront. From where she stood she had a clear view of his
mooring.

She had said goodbye, he goodnight. Did that mean he
expected to see her again? Maybe not; maybe his choice
of word had no significance. Certainly it would be better
if they didn't re-encounter each other. She would never
be able to face him without feeling acutely embarrassed.

His tall figure came into sight, moving with a leisurely
stride and trailing a long black shadow on the moonlit
ground.

At one point he paused to look down from the edge of
the quay and she wondered if he was watching a shoal of
fish swimming between the boats. The water in the harbour was astonishingly clear, quite different from the
murky depths of other harbours she had visited.

After a little he moved on until he came to her boat.
With the accustomed ease of a man to whom a boat is as
much a part of everyday life as the car to a non-seafaring
man, he used her boat as a bridge to his own. Having
loosed the tow rope, he did not start the engine but began
to row.

Admittedly the water in the harbour was calm, and he
had the advantage of far more powerful arms and shoulders, but she could see there was no comparison between
his handling of the oars and her inexpert efforts.

For some moments after she had lost sight of him, she
remained at the railing, surveying the silent village and
the ruined windmill on top of the promontory to the north
of the harbour. She was just turning to go inside when she
heard his engine start up, gradually changing from a
drone to a purr until the sound of it was lost altogether.

Not feeling in the least sleepy, she went inside and
switched on the bedside lamp and the thing which protected her from mosquitoes while she was sleeping. She
had heard other tourists complain that they were covered
with bites because their holiday houses lacked mosquito
screens at the windows and they couldn't stand the smell

caused by burning green spirals of insect-repellant material. Andrew, the owner of her flat, had solved the problem by importing gadgets such as the one near her bed. Loaded with a pastille, it plugged into a socket outlet and, although whatever odour it gave off was undetectable to her nostrils, it effectively kept the mosquitoes at bay.

As she took off the sweater and shirt, she noticed the label at the back of the collar. The shirt was by Hilditch & Key, Shirtmakers since 1899, Jermyn Street, London. Puzzled, she looked for a label in the sweater and was even more startled to see that it came from N. Peal, the cashmere shop in Burlington Arcade, one of London's most expensive shopping places.

She took off the white linen shorts. They were labelled Saint Laurent Rive Gauche.

To afford clothes of this order, at some time in his jack-of-all-trades career Dion must have been earning a great deal of money. Unless—unpalatable thought—they were presents from a wealthy woman with whom he had the kind of relationship which Valissa had always thought even more degrading than those between girls and much older men.

Turning back the cover on her bed, she unzipped the matching case which contained the pillow and her night-dress, a cool shift of blue and white lawn. Then she went to brush her teeth and wash.

Although it was after two o'clock by the time she climbed into bed, it was a long time before she slept. She could still feel Dion's kisses on her mouth and throat, and the touch of his hands on her body. Had she felt the same total abandon when Nick had caressed her? It was too long ago to remember her feelings exactly. She had been so much younger then, a dreamy nineteen-year-old, the sensual side of her nature not fully developed.

In fact, until tonight she hadn't considered that she was a particularly sensual person except in liking sweet scents, and good food, and the feel of a pure silk shirt; and she had always enjoyed stroking the chocolate-brown fur of Rangoon, Elizabeth Barclay's Burmese cat.

But never before had she lain in bed aching with long-ing to be stroked herself, to feel a man's practised hands exploring the soft curves of her body.

It was Dion's fault that she was in this restless, strung-up state. From the moment he had swung her off her feet on the jetty, his effect on her senses had been disturbingly potent. She wished she had never set eyes on the man. It would have been better to have rowed until her palms were raw, or spent the night huddled in her bathing towel on some inaccessible stretch of beach, than to have her well-ordered existence turned upside down by the virile good looks of a Greek island Romeo.

She awoke very early. As soon as it was sufficiently light, she walked up the hill road, past the village's one rather grand house with a magnificent cypress tree in the garden, to have a pre-breakfast bathe in the cove on the other side of the promontory.

When she had taken off the bandages to inspect the state of her palms, she had found them in a better state than she had expected. If protected by waterproof dressings in the sea and the shower, and by rubber gloves while washing her smalls, they looked as if it wouldn't be more than a day or two before there was little to show for what she had been through the night before.

On the way back from the beach, she stopped at the bakery for a loaf of oven-warm bread. Then after shampooing her hair under the shower, she washed out yesterday's tee-shirt and Dion's shirt. Hung on the line across the unshaded part of her roof terrace, they would soon be ready for ironing. She made herself a pot of coffee, and had her breakfast of fresh bread with butter and honey sitting in the sun in a dry bikini.

Anna came early that morning, obviously eager to hear the full story of Valissa's misadventure. To this end she had brought her friend Maria who spoke some English and could interpret her questions and the English girl's answers.

'Do you know the man Dionysios?' Valissa asked them, when she had described what had happened and the time she had arrived back.

After some consultation, both women shook their heads.

Valissa explained that some time in the next day or two he would come for his clothes which she had arranged to leave in Anna's keeping.

The Greek woman nodded, indicating that she would press his shirt as soon as it was ready for ironing. She would also direct him to the beach if he wished to see Thespinis Cornford again.

'No, I shall not be at the beach. I am taking a taxi to Gaios,' Valissa told Maria.

Loggos did not have a resident taxi-driver, but there was one at Lakka, at the northern end of the island, who could be contacted if whoever required his services was not in too much of a hurry.

When he arrived, he already had a couple of passengers so Valissa sat in front. Soon they were speeding along the island's principal road through the inland villages of Magazia, Bogdanatika and Makratika.

Between the villages most of the countryside was given over to groves of very tall, often grotesquely shaped olive trees, some of which were five hundred years old, having been planted in the time when Paxos had been under the suzerainty of Venice.

The couple in the back of the taxi had been to the island many times, and the husband volunteered the information that their Venetian overlords had encouraged the Paxiots to plant olives by giving twelve gold sequins, the coins of the time, for every hundred trees established.

'I believe there are now about three hundred thousand olives on Paxos, and the oil is considered the finest in Greece,' he told Valissa. 'My wife and I always take a five-litre can of it home with us.'

On arriving in Gaios, they invited her to have coffee with them in one of the two main pavement cafés in the waterfront *platia*. They then boarded a caique which was taking visitors to see the rugged west coast, and Valissa began a pleasant potter.

On one corner of the *platia*, not far from the two great stone slabs on which, for a hundred and fifty years, the fishermen of Gaios had been displaying their catches of mullet, dogfish, eels, crayfish and crabs, there was a shop selling fashions and gold and silver jewellery.

Valissa spent some time bending over the show-counters
filled with gold ornaments. Recently Elizabeth Barclay,
chief assistant to Valissa's employer, had returned from a
visit to Kuwait during which she had been taken round
the gold market. She had told Valissa that the Kuwaiti
goldsmiths never worked with metal of less than twenty-
two carats, and would think very poorly of English nine-
carat adornments.

Evidently the Greeks took a similar view. They used
fourteen carat gold, and in this shop none of the objects
was price-tagged. When she asked the cost of a chain, the
shopkeeper weighed it and worked out the price on his
calculator. Obviously his prices varied according to the
fluctuating value of gold bullion.

From him she learned that what she had always called
a Greek key pattern was, here, known as the Maiandros
design, being a stylised form of the meandering river of
that name in Asia Minor.

Other recurring motifs were the dolphin, the owl and
the goat, and what she most longed to buy was a ring in
the form of a ram's head with tightly curled horns. It was
the only one of its kind in the shop, being more delicately
fashioned than the other goat's head rings, and without
their decoration of coloured enamel which she felt would
eventually rub off and spoil their appearance.

However, when the shopkeeper told her the price, re-
gretfully she had to shake her head and tell him it was
more than she could afford.

About half an hour later, in another shop, she did succumb to the lure of a bark-pleated blue cheesecloth dress
with shoestring shoulder ties and a band of cotton crochet,
dyed to match the material, across the décolletage.

It was rather an unnecessary buy considering that her
holiday was already more than half over, and that the
clothes she had brought with her had proved more than
adequate to her needs.

Andrew, her flat's owner, had warned her that Paxos
night-life was very informal, and Susan, his girl-friend, had
complained that it was *too* informal because even the short
cotton voile evening dresses she had bought on a trip to the
West Indies looked out of place on the Greek island.

However, as Valissa had not come to Paxos for the night-life but rather for long days of sunshine, she had not packed anything eveningy, and she thought it might well be next year before she christened her new dress. But even if she didn't wear it immediately, it was the kind of simple, undating garment which would be 'no ill store', as her grandmother's Norfolk-born cleaning woman had used to remark of things put by for future use.

Having spent about an hour looking for small presents for her closest friends, and exploring the back streets and alleys, she decided to have another drink before finding her way to the nearest bathing place.

She had ordered a thirst-quenching fruit juice, and was sitting in the shade of one of the many coloured sunbrellas which sprouted like a patch of exotic mushrooms over all that part of the *platia* occupied by the adjoining pavement cafés, when a man said, '*Kalimera, Thespinis.*'

Had she not recognised the voice, she would have assumed the words were addressed to someone else. But it had a timbre which was unmistakable and, even before she turned her head, she knew who was standing behind her.

'*Kalimera, Kyrie Dionysios,*' she said, rather breathlessly. '*Sas enohlo?*'

She knew it was a question, but not what it meant.

'That's not part of my basic Greek, I'm afraid,' she said, mustering her self-possession and managing a smile.

'I was asking if I was disturbing you.'

Politeness obliged her to shake her head, and reply with a phrase which had stayed in her mind after she had spent part of the flight to Corfu memorising a few essential words and expressions.

'*Kathiste, parakalo.*'

As Dion accepted her invitation to sit down, the waiter arrived with her drink.

'You can't want that bilious-looking stuff,' said Dion, looking with disfavour at the too vividly orange contents of the tall glass. He spoke in Greek to the waiter, who shrugged, grinned, nodded and left them.

'The proper thing to drink is *ouzo*. Haven't you tried it yet?'

'No, and really I wanted something thirst-quenching rather than intoxicating.'

'*Ouzo* will quench your thirst, and one measure isn't too intoxicating. You can't go back to England without trying our national aperitif. Actually *ouzo* is only a form of a drink which one finds all round the Mediterranean. In the Middle East they call it arrack, in France two well known brands are Pernod and Ricard, and in Spain it's anis. They're all distantly related to absinthe, but without containing the wormwood which used to make absinthe drinkers suicidally depressed. *Ouzo* has the reverse effect. It makes one agreeably euphoric.'

'I thought you did your shopping in Loggos,' Valissa said, after a pause.

'Mostly I do. But as my place is more or less equidistant, sometimes I come here instead. How do you feel today? Recovered?' There was a faint glint in his eye which suggested he wasn't thinking only of her ordeal at sea.

She looked away. 'Yes, thank you ... completely recovered.'

'Having resorted to the infallible panacea for all feminine ills from headache to heartbreak, I see,' he said, indicating the parcel containing her new dress. 'What have you been buying?'

'Just a cheap dress. Nothing extravagant.'

'With your figure you don't need extravagant clothes. Only a woman who has lost her figure, or never had one, needs to put a lot of money on her back.'

'There's nothing wrong with your figure, but you seem to spend a great deal of money on your back,' was her light riposte.

'What do you mean?' His voice had a curiously sharp edge.

'I couldn't help noticing the labels in the clothes you lent me. I consider myself quite well paid, but I can't afford to shop at Saint Laurent or in the Burlington Arcade.'

There was no mistaking the flicker of annoyance in his eyes. Clearly he would have preferred her to be less observant.

The waiter brought two glasses containing *ouzo*, and

two of iced water. He also set down a dish of olives and small chunks of *feta* impaled on wooden toothpicks.

Both Dion and Valissa thanked him, and he replied with '*Parakolo*' before moving on to another table. As she had already discovered, in Greece a word of thanks always elicited a 'Please' in response.

The hint of a frown still lingered between Dion's brows. He said, 'Those clothes were handed down to me by a rich man I worked for last year.'

'Oh, I see. Then I absolve you of extravagance,' said Valissa. But she had the unpleasant suspicion that his explanation, if not a lie, somehow fell short of the truth.

She herself had told very few lies in her life, and never with the ease with which some people could make a falsehood sound plausible. Now she thought she detected in Dion's manner the discomfiture of a man who is not a liar by nature, but whose last remark had not been truthful. Could it be that the clothes had been bought for him by a rich woman?

She watched him pour half his iced water into the glass containing *ouzo* where the two formed a cloudy white mixture. He then drank the rest of the water, before raising the other glass to her. '*Ya sas!*'

Valissa repeated his actions. She found the diluted *ouzo* quite palatable, but her taste-buds didn't thrill to it.

Dion offered her the dish of olives. 'These appetisers don't compare with the *mezés* you would be given in the best *kafénions* in Athens. There you might have a little *brik*, which is red caviare, or perhaps some *taramasalata*, a preparation of fish roes, or a small bowl of *chachik* which is cucumber with yoghurt and garlic. Having said that, I have to admit that Greece is not a country to delight the gourmet as France does; and here in Paxos the food is well below average. Almost everything is fried, except the very bad mass-produced *moussaka*, and there are only four or five other dishes to choose from.'

'I think you're too critical,' she answered. 'I haven't eaten out much yet, but with good bread, fresh fish, excellent tomatoes and the most deliciously creamy yoghurt which I've ever tasted, I have no complaints about the food here.'

'You may have, when you've tried more taverna meals. In Gaios, the best place to eat is Dodo's where they do quite a good pizza, and not far from here, as the boat goes, there's Pan and Theo's place at Mogonisi.'

'I'll bear that in mind.'

Why did she feel a little pang of disappointment because he hadn't added something such as 'Let me take you to one of them this evening'?

To feel deflated was absurd when she had already made up her mind to avoid any further contact with him, and had come to Gaios today in pursuance of that resolution.

With uncanny percipience, he said, 'If you were five years older, I'd take you to Mogonisi tonight and give you a lesson in *syrtaki* dancing.' His glance took in her slim figure, clad in a cotton top and tiered Indian skirt. His strange eyes returned to her face. 'But in the circumstances, I don't think that would be a good idea.'

'In what circumstances?'

He crossed long brown legs, and she noticed the sinews in his thighs. But his ankles were slim, and, in dark city socks, would look elegant.

'Valissa, I'm thirty-three, and I've led a somewhat dissolute life. You're what? Nineteen? Maybe twenty. That's not a good combination.'

She took another drink of *ouzo*.

'No . . . it wouldn't be,' she agreed.

Did she really look as young as that? Maybe without any make-up, her face brown and a scatter of freckles on her nose, she could pass for a nineteen-year-old to a man in his early thirties.

'What do you mean by "a dissolute life"?' she asked.

'Perhaps that was overstating it. But I'm certainly a lot more experienced than you are. And even if I were not, I should think twice about poaching on someone else's territory. Before you woke up from that bad dream you had at the cottage, you called out "Nick" several times. I could be wrong, but I have the feeling Nick is the reason you've come on holiday on your own.'

In a manner of speaking, he was right. It was because she had lost Nick, and committed herself to her work with a single-minded dedication which Elizabeth Barclay thought unnatural, that she was in Paxos by herself.

She said, 'I think what triggered that nightmare was a paragraph in my *Travellers' Guide to Corfu and the Other Ionian Islands*. It warns people not to swim far out to sea, or to bathe where very deep water comes right up to the shore, as it does on the west coast of this island. I remember one bit very clearly. "Sharks are very rare, but the myth that they are small and harmless dies tragically every year with one or two unfortunate bathers somewhere in the Mediterranean." That sentence was lurking at the back of my mind while I was rowing in the storm, and later I dreamt that Nick and I were trapped on the cliffs on the west coast, and he was determined to swim for help. I was begging him not to attempt it when you woke me up.'

'You're in love with him?'

She gave a little sad shake of her head. 'I *was* in love with him. We were going to be married, but then he was killed in a ghastly pile-up on a motorway.'

On the rare occasions when she was forced to explain about Nick, the usual reaction was a look of embarrassment, an awkward expression of sympathy, and a hurried change of subject.

Dion's reaction was different. He reached for her hands and, leaning close to her, pressed them between his larger ones.

'Poor little Valissa! That's a hellish thing to happen at your age. No wonder you have a forlorn look.'

'D-do I?' she said, a little unsteadily.

She would not have thought that his eyes—usually gleaming with sardonic humour—could show so much tender concern, and she found it oddly moving.

'Not all the time. But when I caught sight of you wandering through town earlier on, you did. I don't think coming on holiday by yourself was a good idea. Haven't you got any girl friends you could have teamed up with?'

'None whose holiday dates fitted with mine. I don't mind being alone. I like it.'

The waiter came by, and Dion asked for the bill. When Valissa would have shared it, he said, 'Don't be ridiculous.'

She reached for her beach bag and parcel. 'Well ...
thank you for introducing me to *ouzo*. Your clothes are
with Anna whenever it's convenient for you to collect
them. Goodbye.'

He had also risen to his feet, ducking out from under
the sunbrella in order to be able to stand at his full height.
'Where are you off to now? Back to Loggos?'

'No, I'm going to stroll along there'—with a gesture
towards the quay—'and find somewhere to bathe before
lunch.'

'The first bay is only a few minutes' walk away. There's
a taverna above the second bay where you can get a pass-
able snack.'

'Is there? Oh, good. 'Bye.' She made to walk away
then, on impulse, checked and turned back to him. 'By
the way, you're not a very good judge of women's ages. I
was nineteen when Nick and I were engaged, but that
was some time ago. I'm twenty-four now.'

Without waiting to see how he took this information,
she walked swiftly along the aisle between the rows of
tables and, near where the ferries to Mogonisi and
Antipaxos had been berthed earlier, turned right along
the long waterfront.

Why had she told him her real age? Wasn't he likely to
take it as a tacit invitation to shelve his scruples and
regard her as fair game? And if he did think that, would
he be so far wrong? Deep down, wasn't she longing for
him to pursue her?

No ... no ... absolutely not! Valissa apostrophised
herself, as she hurried away from the *platia*, the hem of
her cotton skirt swirling with the briskness of her pace.

Now noon, it was a hot time of day to be walking
quickly, but she did not pause until, near the entrance to
the harbour, she came to a statue of a man with a mous-
tache, holding aloft what looked at first glance like a
paintbrush, and wearing what seemed to be a cummer-
bund and baggy knee-length trousers. There was an in-
scription on the plinth, but it was in Greek and therefore
she couldn't read it.

All the time she had been walking, people on scooters
and motorbikes had been buzzing past her in both direc-

itons, the quay being also the roadway. The sound of yet another small motorbike didn't cause her to turn her head, even when it stopped close by.

Only when Dion said, 'That's Anemoyanis, the sailor who set fire to the Turkish flagship during the war of 1821,' did she turn a startled face to his. He strolled closer. 'Do you carry your passport about with you?'

'Not always. I brought it with me today in case I should be asked for it if I wanted to cash a traveller's cheque.'

'Which in Gaios is done at the ironmongery shop, by a woman known as the Black Widow,' he said, with a smile. 'May I look at your passport?'

'If you wish,' she agreed perplexedly. With her billfold, it was in a zipped pocket in the lining of her beach bag. She produced it and handed it to him.

'Thank you.' He turned to the pages which bore her photograph and description.

The photograph, a coloured one, showed her fully made up, with a sophisticated hairdo, and wearing a suit from Options, the women's department on the third floor of Austin Reed's Regent Street shop where she went for many of her working clothes.

'So you really are twenty-four—or will be in two months' time,' he said, looking from her date of birth to the photograph. 'I was just checking. You wouldn't be the first female to bend the truth about her age. And this is how you look in your natural habitat. Who would have thought it?'

'I imagine most people look rather different on holiday,' she said coolly, holding out her hand for the passport.

He returned it to her. 'Possibly.' Walking back to where he had propped the motorbike, he swung a leg over the saddle. Having settled himself astride the small machine, he said, 'Hop on.'

'W-where are you going?'

'I'm coming with you for a swim, and then we'll have lunch together.' When she stayed where she was, her expression reflecting her indecision, he added, with a glint of mockery, 'If you hadn't wished to pursue our acquaintance, you wouldn't have mentioned your age to me, Valissa. Come on, I want to cool off.'

Not at all sure that she was doing the right thing, but moved by an urge to enjoy the moment and never mind the consequences, she mounted the pillion. With the beach bag on her lap, and her hands holding him by the waist, they set off. After travelling only a short distance, Dion stopped where the road overlooked a small inviting bay of clear blue-green water.

'Step off on your left foot,' he warned her. 'I've seen several women with nasty burns on their ankles caused by accidentally coming into contact with the hot exhaust pipe.'

A few minutes later they were standing on the beach, exchanging smiles with the few other people already there.

It took Dion only seconds to be ready for the water. He pulled off his shirt, stepped out of his shorts and, clad in the briefest of black trunks, stood waiting for her to finish fastening her sea shoes. That done, she removed her skirt and top under which she was wearing a cotton bikini to match her eyes.

It was the scantiest of the four bikinis she had with her, the bottom part consisting of two triangles joined by narrow bands across the hips for maximum tanning. The even skimpier triangles of the top part were only suitable for someone with small firm breasts in no need of uplift. Valissa had been pleased when the bouncier bosom of her plump days had been reduced to its present proportions. But now, with Dion's eyes on her, she wondered if he found her shape disappointing and preferred more voluptuous contours.

Side by side they walked into the sea. His soles must be tougher than hers as the stones did not make him hobble.

'Mm ... heavenly!' she murmured when, at waist depth, she turned towards the beach and sank slowly backwards into the lukewarm water.

She saw Dion inhale, his deep chest expanding as he drew in a long breath of air. With hardly a splash he disappeared under the surface, eventually to reappear quite a long way away by some rocks. Obviously keeping a wary eye out for sea-urchins, he climbed carefully out of the water, his tanned body glistening in the sun, the thinly-fleshed muscles rippling under the bronze-coloured skin.

Nearly naked, he looked even more magnificent than when he was merely stripped to the waist. Everyone on the beach was gazing at him, she noticed, but he seemed unaware of being watched. For a few moments longer he stood watching a yacht out at sea before taking another deep breath to dive cleanly back into the water.

It was so clear that she saw him swimming towards her under the surface several yards before he reached her. She hoped he wasn't the type of man who found it amusing to grab girls' ankles which, competent swimmer though she was, she had always detested having done to her. But he didn't. He came up beside her, grinning, shaking his curly head like a dog.

'This is the life, eh?'

'Yes, it's glorious,' she agreed happily, but with the mental reservation that, blissful as all this was for two weeks, or even a month, it wasn't enough to content her month in and month out.

Lotus-eating was lovely—on holiday. It wasn't a way of life; or at least not for her. She knew she would need more stimulus than was to be found on this small island.

They stayed in the water for a long time, then basked on a flat piece of rock. Presently she left him lying there and went to change into a dry bikini. Her Indian skirt had a shirred waist which made it a useful changing tent. All the three other women on the beach had discarded their bikini bras and probably thought her very prudish to change under cover.

But her own feeling was that she did not want to display her bare breasts to everyone, only to a lover, in private. How unexciting, as was the case with one of the girls—the other two had no men with them—to lie stretched out by one's lover or husband, one's nudity of no interest to him.

I should want the sight of my bosom to make him want to make love to me, thought Valissa, towelling her hair. But look what happened to ankles, after short skirts came in. I suppose breasts will go the same way, given enough exposure.

She saw Dion rise to his feet with the indolent suppleness of a panther.

As he joined her, she asked, 'Have you something dry to change into?'

'Only my shorts. I'll borrow your towel, if I may. I've left mine in the boat which I've swopped with a friend of mine. He wanted my boat for a couple of days, and I've taken over his bike. I hope it's a fair exchange. I don't want to find myself walking you home tonight.'

So he meant to spend all day and evening with her. And then what? All night as well?

What have I got myself into? she wondered, with a tremor of apprehension.

CHAPTER THREE

They had lunch outside the taverna which Dion had mentioned to her; a simple meal of an omelette and salad with bread and wine.

Still taking care not to burn, Valissa wore a short cotton wrap over her bikini.

'It's an unusual name—Valissa. I don't think I've heard it before,' he said, as they began eating.

'My grandfather suggested it to my parents. His mother's surname was Vallis, a corruption of de Valois, which suggests that her father's forebears came from the Duchy of Valois. Perhaps they were refugees from the French Revolution.'

She was going to ask him his surname, but he forestalled her by saying, 'Where do your parents live?'

'They died when I was a baby. I don't remember them. My grandparents brought me up. Now that he's on his own, my grandfather lives in a small apartment in what used to be a country mansion and is now converted into flats for elderly people with some private means. It's a very nice place. He can have his own furniture there, and there's a communal dining-room and a drawing-room where the residents can mix if they wish to. It's quite close to London, so I see him every weekend. Your parents? Are they alive?'

'Unfortunately not. My mother died when I was fifteen; and my father, who was considerably older, a few years later.'

'Have you any brothers and sisters?'

'One sister, and innumerable aunts and uncles and cousins. Too many,' he added, with a wry grin.

'I should like to be part of a large family. When my grandfather dies, I shan't have any close relations.'

'You can remedy that by having children. Or doesn't that solution appeal to you?'

'It did at one time. Now . . . I don't know.'

'It would be a pity to waste the genes which have made you a beautiful girl.' He leaned back and drank some white wine, appraising her face and what he could see of her body. 'An exceptionally beautiful girl.'

The frank desire in his eyes brought a rosy tint to the deepening brown of her cheeks. Did he mean it, or was it a line he had found effective in the past?

His next remark was unexpected. He said, 'Sometimes, when I see how uncomfortably crowded Europe is becoming except in a place such as this which is not too easy to reach, I think it would be a splendid idea if people had to have a licence to reproduce—and the licences were only issued to couples with certain qualifications.'

'What kind of qualifications?'

'Beauty or brains ... proven creativity or craftsmanship. Selective breeding works with animals. Why not with people?'

'Because handsome, intelligent parents don't always have bright, good-looking children. As George Bernard Shaw wrote to Isadora Duncan when she suggested having a child by him to combine her looks with his brains— Supposing it had my looks and your brains? Anyway, I'm not sure that the qualities you've mentioned are as important as kindness and tolerance, and how can they be measured?'

They were still goodhumouredly arguing when their plates and the wine bottle were empty.

Dion signalled the waiter. 'Coffee and brandy?' he asked her.

'Coffee, please. No brandy for me. Even wine, in this heat, makes me sleepy.'

'Then we'll find a quiet spot where you can sleep. Why not? A holiday is for doing as one pleases when one pleases. The only trouble is that the beaches here are not very comfortable for lying on without a straw mat or an air-bed.'

'Are there no sandy beaches at all?'

'Only on Antipaxos. Voutoumi bay there is like a Caribbean beach—fine sand on the beach and the sea bed. It's usually fairly crowded with day visitors, and the beach bar is scruffy, but, providing one takes one's own lunch, it's a good place to spend a day. We could go there tomorrow, if you like.'

The return of the waiter, making some remark in Greek, saved Valissa from having to commit herself.

While they were drinking their coffee, she said, 'You mentioned Caribbean beaches. Were you speaking from hearsay or experience?'

'I have been to the Caribbean.'

Was it her imagination, or was his tone somewhat guarded? And was there a whiff of a red herring about the speed with which he asked her if she had visited Lakka, the most northerly of the island's villages.

'Not yet. I saw it from the ferry on the evening I arrived from Corfu. Several of the passengers landed there. It looked much the same as Loggos, but a little larger. Is there something special to see there?'

'Not really. It has more shops than Loggos, but not as many as Gaios. I think you would find it more interesting to make the trip to Parga, on the mainland.'

It was on the tip of Valissa's tongue to say that, with only a few days left, she thought she would rather relax than go on excursions. But something made her leave the remark unspoken, and later she was glad she had held her tongue.

Presently they went for another spin on the bike, the road winding past several holiday villas and giving a glimpse of the cottage colony of the Paxos Beach Hotel.

By the time Dion braked to a standstill, the breeziness of motorbike riding had dispelled her slight drowsiness earlier and she was eager to swim again.

Somewhat to her surprise, and although they had their bathing place to themselves for most of the long afternoon, he did not kiss her or touch her, as she had expected he might.

When they weren't in the water, but were clambering about on the rocks or lying in the sun, drying off, he seemed genuinely curious to find out her views on various subjects. Perhaps this, also, was a technique he had found successful with the type of girl who would jib at too rapid a pass.

Although why he should think *I* might jib, considering

the way I let him kiss me at the cottage, I can't imagine, she thought perplexedly.

The heat of the day was mellowing when they returned to Gaios.

'I want to fill up with petrol,' said Dion, over his shoulder, as he rode past the end of the *platia* and on towards the quay where her ferry from Corfu had berthed.

However, before he reached that point, he turned down an alley to the left. A few yards along it, he stopped, and asked her to dismount.

'Where's the pump?' she asked, as she obeyed him.

'There isn't one.' Having dismounted himself, and pulled the bike on to its prop, he grinned at her baffled expression.

Then he disappeared through an open doorway. She heard him speaking his own language, and another man replying. A few minutes later he reappeared carrying a watering-can from which he proceeded to fill the bike's tank, the cap of which was concealed under the driver's seat.

'There we are; that should ensure that, if we do break down on the way home, it won't be for lack of juice,' he said. 'Next, I think we should top ourselves up with a little more *ouzo*.'

They rode back to the *platia* where he parked the bike by the church which stood in the centre of it.

People who had spent the day at Mogonisi were disembarking from the ferry and making for the café tables, other tourists were buying supplies from the food and vegetable shops, and the old men of the village had emerged from their whitewashed houses and were ambling about, studying the tourists and chatting to each other.

'This time of the evening when people congregate in the square is known as the *volta*, or stroll,' said Dion, as they found a free table outside the Café Volcano.

'Like the *paseo* in Spain.'

'Exactly. You've been to Spain?'

'Only once, and it wasn't a holiday, I was working. My firm were doing a holiday house on the Costa Blanca for a Yorkshire millionaire. It was rather a difficult assignment because he and his wife had started life with very little money, and neither of them had any ideas of their own. They gave us complete carte blanche.'

'Doesn't that make it much easier?'

'Oh, no—the reverse. More difficult. If a client says "My favourite colours are apricot and pale blue, and I have a collection of terracotta figures which I want to display", it's much, much easier than when one has nothing to work on.'

'How had he made his fortune, this Yorkshireman?'

'By manufacturing some equipment for supermarkets. I'm not sure what it was, and I'm not certain that he was literally a millionaire. But certainly money was no object with him. "Nothing but the best?" was his watchword, and by that he meant the most expensive. When the house was done it was stunning, but I don't think he was entirely satisfied. Probably he'd been thinking in terms of cut velvet curtains instead of plain linens and cottons, and expensive overstuffed furniture instead of the cane chairs and sofas which are right for that kind of house.'

The waiter arrived.

'I'd rather have an ice than *ouzo*,' said Valissa, before Dion could order. 'And this time it's definitely on me,' she added, when the waiter had gone.

He gave her a considering look, amusement lurking in the depths of his curiously changeable eyes which sometimes looked grey, sometimes golden.

Laughter tugged at the corners of his mouth. 'Very well, if you insist. But I will pay for our supper.'

While she was eating her ice, he noticed the Gemini ring she was wearing.

'You didn't buy that here, did you?'

'No, only this little dolphin'—showing him the ring on the little finger of her right hand. 'Which reminds me, there was a double dolphin ring which I thought I would buy to go with this one. They're all ridiculously cheap.'

'If you've seen another ring you like, I should buy it at once, if I were you. The high season is already over, and the shopkeepers' stocks are running low and won't be replenished till next year. No one comes to Paxos in winter. It's wet, and in January and February the temperature sometimes drops below freezing point. But if it weren't for the rains in winter, we shouldn't be as green in the summer.'

Presently he accompanied her to the shop where she had seen the double dolphin ring. It was no longer there, and Valissa thought she might have seen one like it in the shop which also sold gold jewellery, including the coveted ram's head.

As she entered, a step ahead of Dion, the shopkeeper recognised her. He moved to the showcase containing it. 'You wish to try the ring again, *madame?*'

Although most of the foreigners on the island seemed to be English, quite a few of the shopkeepers used the French form of address.

She shook her head. 'No—no, thank you. I'm looking for a silver ring like this one, but with two dolphins.'

'I am sorry, I cannot help you. One dolphin—yes. Two—no.'

'Oh, well, never mind,' she said, smiling. Her glance strayed to the gold rings showcase.

'Which was the ring you tried on before?' asked Dion.

'One of those, but it was much more expensive and I can't really afford it.'

'But the gold is fourteen carat, better than you will find in England, *madame*,' the shopkeeper said persuasively.

'And gold is always a good investment,' added Dion. 'A chain which I bought for my sister some years ago would now cost twice as much.'

'Yes, I know, but my big investment is my flat in London, and with mortgage rates at their present level, I can't run to a holiday abroad *and* a gold ring,' she said lightly. 'Goodbye'—this to the shopkeeper.

Dion said something to him in Greek.

'What did you say to him?' she asked, when they had left the shop.

'That women have been known to change their minds. Shall we stretch our legs for half an hour? It's a little early to eat yet.'

'Yes . . . a good idea,' she agreed.

But as they strolled along the waterfront in the direction of the former Residency, she was not altogether convinced that Dion's remark to the shopkeeper had been what he claimed it had been. She knew that travel couriers frequently received a rake-off by recommending holiday-makers to patronise certain shops and avoid others. Could it be that what Dion had actually said had been to the effect that he would encourage her to buy the ring, but would expect a percentage of the profit?

Why do I keep having these unworthy suspicions about him? she wondered uncomfortably. He rescued me from the storm. He could have seduced me, but he didn't. So far, he's behaved impeccably. And yet I don't altogether trust him. Why not? What is it about him which makes me doubtful?

The Residency was the most impressive building in Gaios, a three-storey edifice topped by two attic pavilions linked by a wall pierced with arches.

'It's used by the harbour police now,' Dion told her, as they stood looking up at the green-shuttered, balconied façade. The design of the balcony railing reminded Valissa of Regency balconies in England.

'Why was it built? Did Paxos belong to Britain once?' she asked.

'Yes, this island fell to the British in 1814, and the Treaty of Paris, after the Battle of Waterloo, established the Union of Ionian Islands under the protection of Britain. There was a Lord High Commissioner on Kerkyra—which is what Greeks call Corfu—and Residents on the six smaller islands. It wasn't until fifty years later that the islands became part of Greece again. Paxos is now a sub-province of Kerkyra.'

'You're very well informed,' she said thoughtfully.

'It surprises you that the grandson of a fisherman should have a little education?'

'It surprises me that, with so much education, you have no definite occupation,' she answered, wondering if the outspoken comment would offend him.

But he only grinned. 'I get by. A man who can turn his hand to most things, and isn't afraid of hard work, need never starve in the Western world.'

'No, probably not, but he'll never make much money either.'

'Is money important to you, Valissa? Do you dream of being rich?' Dion asked.

'No, but I shouldn't care to be poor—or not to be sure where my next year's income was coming from.'

'The man you were going to marry: how did he make his living?'

'He hadn't finished his training. He was going to be a painter . . . an artist.'

'That's a very precarious profession,' Dion said dryly.

'Yes, but Nick was enormously talented, and I would have worked as well until he'd established himself. Also he had an income from some money left to him by his grandmother.'

'Enough income to live on?'

'Just about. We'd have had to be careful.'

'Would you have married him without the security of that income?'

'But of course,' she retorted, rather indignantly. 'I loved him. I would have married him if he hadn't had a penny.'

'But he had, so you can't be certain. I'm not saying you wouldn't have done so. I suppose there are women who will throw in their lot with a man who has nothing to offer, but not many of them, I fancy.'

'There are women who will marry a man knowing that, within a few years, they will have to pay a terrible price for their happiness,' she said, thinking of Mary O'Hara, the singer and harpist, whose albums were among her favourite records.

'And many more for whom a man is just a meal-ticket,' was his somewhat clipped answer. 'Preferably to a five-star restaurant.'

The cynicism in his voice made her wonder if he had once been in love with a girl who had ditched him for someone with money.

'Now you're making me feel uncomfortable about letting you pay for my supper. Why don't we go Dutch?' she said lightly. 'Then you'll know I have no ulterior motive for being nice to you.'

He caught her lightly by the arm and swung her to face him.

'Are you going to be nice to me, Valissa?'

Warm colour crept up from her throat as he looked

down into her face, a teasing half-smile on his mouth, but a different gleam in his eyes.

'I . . . is that why you're being nice to me?' she asked unsteadily.

'I want to make love to you—yes. But only if you want it too.'

'I . . . we've only just met. The day before yesterday I didn't know you.'

'So? One can be attracted to a person from the moment of shaking hands. An hour or two later one can want very much to be in bed with them.'

'I know men often feel that. It's not usually so rapid for my sex.'

He laughed. 'It is, you know. There's no difference. Can you deny that last night, when I kissed you, you enjoyed it?'

'That isn't fair. I was half asleep . . . upset . . . confused.'

His fingers caressed her bare arm. 'You were adorable,' he said softly. 'Soft . . . pliant . . . eager. Everything a woman should be in a man's arms. I don't know how I tore myself away. I've regretted it ever since. If I hadn't believed you to be much younger, we should still be there, making love. Let's forget staying for supper in Gaios. Let's go back to my place, or your place. I'm not hungry. I only want you.'

His low, urgent tone and the ardour which darkened his eyes were scarcely less overwhelming than if he had seized her in his arms. A few other men had made passes at her, but never like this. Never in a public place, not caring who overheard them.

'No . . . no . . . I can't,' she protested. 'I know I responded to you last night, but I'm not really like that at all. I couldn't go to bed with a man until I knew him much better than I know you, Dion. I mean, we . . . we're virtually strangers.'

'How can you say that? We've just spent all afternoon finding out about each other. I think on most of the important issues we are very much en rapport.'

'Perhaps . . . but it's still much too soon. Barely twenty-four hours since we first set eyes on each other.'

His hand dropped from her arm and he stepped back. 'All right, I'll give you more time. But it's only prolonging the inevitable. I think you know that as well as I do.' He glanced at his watch. 'It's still early to eat. Let's go and watch the flotilla berthing.'

The flotilla was a fleet of yachts which, cruising in the Ionian under the leadership of a professional helmsman, afforded an enjoyable fortnight's holiday to people with varying degrees of sailing proficiency who preferred to be part of a group rather than to cruise independently.

Valissa had seen them earlier, when they were still out at sea, and Dion had told her about them. Now the first boats to put in were berthed close alongside each other, and soon they would all be at their moorings near a bar which was already doing a brisk business in glasses of beer and gin-and-tonics.

While she and Dion were watching, someone said, 'Hello, Valissa. How's your holiday going?'

She turned. 'Oh . . . Christopher! Hello.'

She recognised him immediately: the man with whom she had had coffee after dining in Gaios on her own, the night before last. But since then she had forgotten his existence, and had had to think twice to remember his name.

Hoping he hadn't noticed her slight hesitation, she said, 'I'm having a fine time, thank you. And you? Are you enjoying yourself?'

'Yes, but more so if you'll have supper with me.'

Evidently he hadn't realised that she and the tall Greek were together. Neither she nor Dion had spoken in the previous few minutes, and Christopher must have spotted her among the onlookers and thought she was still by herself.

It was as he invited her to supper that Dion turned and appraised him. They could not have been more dissimilar; the Greek with his thick cap of curls, and his dark skin and muscular frame, and the tall but much slighter Englishman whose fair skin was still at the red stage, and whose hair was fair and so fine that it kept slipping across his forehead in a boyish forelock.

'I'm afraid I can't, Christopher. I'm dining with Dion,'

she explained. 'I don't know either of your surnames, so I can't introduce you properly.'

'Carter,' Christopher supplied. 'How do you do?'—offering his hand to the other man.

Dion shook it, causing Christopher to wince slightly. Instead of mentioning his own surname—perhaps he had found that it was difficult for foreigners to pronounce it—he said, 'Life is very informal here. I should doubt if many of these people'—indicating the flotilla crews—'know each other by more than their first names. As I have pre-empted the pleasure of dining with Valissa, perhaps you would care to have an aperitif with us,' he added pleasantly.

'Oh, that's very nice of you. Thanks. Are you also on holiday here?' Christopher enquired.

'Yes, but not in the sense of being away from home,' said Dion, as they started to stroll back to the *platia*.

'You're a Paxiot?' Christopher looked surprised. 'You must be the tallest man on the island. Most of the people here are below average height.'

'The older people, yes. Many of them probably didn't have enough to eat while they were growing up. If you look at the young people and children, you'll see that they will be considerably taller than their parents and grandparents.'

At the café Valissa asked for a coffee, Christopher chose beer, and Dion ordered *ouzo*.

'Where are you staying?' he asked the Englishman.

'My parents have rented a house a mile or so up the hill road. There are seven of us altogether . . . my sister and brother-in-law, and their two small children. The others have all been smitten with a touch of what the travel agents call "holiday tummy", so they're having boiled eggs and dry biscuits for supper tonight. Fortunately, I'm unaffected and, having had a long tramp to see the Erimitis cliffs, I feel like a more substantial meal. Have you seen the cliffs yet, Valissa?'

She shook her head. 'Are they very spectacular?'

'Quite impressive, but it's a hot, tiring trek to get there. I should think the best view is from the sea. Would you agree?'—this to Dion.

'Yes, the trip round the west coat by caique is less ex-
hausting—providing there isn't a swell and one is a good
sailor. Whether you are impressed by Erimitis depends on
how many cliffs you have seen before. One interesting
fact about them is that during the last century the villagers
used to fish for swallows from them.'

'*Fish* for swallows?' Valissa echoed.

'With a hook and line, and a fly as bait. In the spring
there would be crowds of swallows round the cliffs, and
the people would catch them with much the same technique as fly-fishing for salmon in Scotland.'

'Good lord, how extraordinary,' said Christopher.

Valissa thought it equally extraordinary that Dion
should know about an élite sport like fly-fishing. Then she
remembered that he had crewed for at least one very rich
man, and must have learned about it from him.

'What a horrible sport,' she said, frowning.

'I doubt if it was merely sport. Presumably they ate
them, like quails. The English used to eat blackbirds,' he
reminded her. 'Would you excuse me for five minutes.
There is someone I want to have a word with. It won't
take long.'

Leaving his *ouzo* unfinished, he walked up the aisle between the tables, turning left at the corner by the *periptero*,
a kiosk selling newspapers, cigarettes and a dozen and
one other things from razor blades to indigestion tablets.

For some minutes Christopher continued to chat about
the island and the November olive harvest.

'I notice there are huge rolls of black nylon netting in
most of the olive groves, and a few have already been
slung beneath the branches to catch the fruit when it
drops,' he told her. Then: 'Where did you meet your
Greek friend?'

Valissa described her mishap with the boat.

'My God! What a frightful experience for you,' was his
concerned reaction. 'The man who hired out the boat
with an unserviced motor ought not to be allowed to get
away with it. Did you insist on a refund?'

'I haven't seen him yet, but it's difficult to take a strong
line when I have about ten words of Greek and he has
twenty of English.'

'I should have thought this chap'—with a nod in the direction taken by Dion—'could have dealt with it for you.'

'I daresay he may say something about it.'

Christopher finished his beer. 'If you don't mind a word of advice, I'd be a little wary of letting Dion become too friendly, if I were you. I imagine you're giving him supper as a more diplomatic return for his help than a straightforward offer of money, which might cause offence. But although he may be an exception, the fact is that a lot of these Mediterranean types have it fixed in their heads that all girls from northern Europe are ... well, pretty permissive, shall I say.'

'Actually Dion is giving me supper, and he isn't the kind of small-town Lothario who's never been farther than Corfu. He's a good deal more travelled than I am,' she responded mildly.

Privately, she found Christopher's avuncular attitude rather irritating, but she realised that he meant well.

'How are you getting back to Loggos?' he asked. 'On the same bus you caught the other night?'

'No, Dion has a motorbike. He'll run me back.'

'I see.' He looked even more dubious. 'It's chilly on the back of a motorbike after dark. If you haven't brought a cardigan with you, you can make that an excuse to take a taxi. Otherwise he might decide to stop on the way, and there are several stretches of road where you'd be a long way from help if you needed it.'

'Really, Christopher, aren't you being excessively alarmist?' she asked crisply. 'If Dion were that sort of man, he had plenty of opportunity to pounce on me at his cottage. Anyone as good-looking as he is doesn't have to force himself on women; besides which, I'm not a naïve girl of sixteen. I've been taking care of myself for quite a number of years now. Oh ... you're back'—as Dion rejoined them.

'I went to borrow a sweater for you to wear riding home tonight. My body will act as a windshield to some extent, but you'll be glad of this as well.' He handed her a pale blue knitted jacket.

'Thank you. How very kind of its owner to lend her

jacket to a stranger.'

He sat down and drank some more *ouzo*. 'It belongs to my very first girl-friend who is now married to someone else, and the mother of two babies.' He looked at Christopher. 'As I overheard Valissa's last remark to you, I gather you had been making the same mistake as I did.'

The Englishman was looking put out. 'I'm afraid I'm not with you,' he said stiffly.

'With her pigtail, and her freckled nose, she looks deceptively young and innocent,' Dion said, smiling at her. 'But if you were to see the photograph of her passport, you'd realise she is actually a sophisticated woman of the world who, in her professional persona, would probably run rings round us both.'

'Really? What is your profession?' Christopher asked, looking startled.

He had told her during their first meeting that he was a solicitor, a junior partner in a firm founded by his great-grandfather. But he had not asked her what she did, perhaps assuming that she had some fairly humdrum office job.

'I'm a designer. I work for Eliot Rutherford.' Then, seeing that the name meant nothing to him, 'He's one of England's top designer-decorators. If your parents live in Cadogan Gardens, you must have passed our showroom in Sloane Street.'

'Possibly. I believe there are several furnishing shops there, aren't there? I can't say I've ever taken a great deal of notice of them.'

'Yes, there are three or four,' she agreed. A gurgle of laughter bubbled up. 'I was visualising Eliot's pained expression if he heard his temple of elegance dismissed as a furnishing shop.'

Dion grinned. 'Takes himself seriously, does he?'

'Very! And not without justification. He *is* a genius in his field.'

Christopher said stuffily, 'It seems a peculiar occupation for a man—choosing wallpapers and so on.'

Valissa said, 'It involves rather more than choosing wallpapers, and it's an occupation which has had some very distinguished practitioners. Robert Adam, for example.'

'Surely he was an architect?'

'Yes, but also a designer-decorator in that he dealt with all the interior details as well as the actual building. I expect you'll take more interest in such things when you marry and have a home of your own, instead of sharing a flat with two other men,' she added.

He appeared to doubt it. 'Possibly.'

Dion rose. 'I think we should eat now, Valissa. See you around, Carter.'

The Englishman responded with an unsmiling nod. Valissa, sensitive to nuances, guessed that he felt some resentment at being addressed by his surname by a man whom he probably regarded as a social inferior.

Not totally charmless, but definitely a bit of a diehard, was her opinion of Christopher.

'A fine upstanding young Englishman,' Dion said blandly, when they had parted from him. 'Where did you run into him?'

She explained.

'Did he try to make a date with you?'

'Yes, but I turned it down.'

'Why? You don't like him?'

'Not well enough to want to spend all my time with him.'

'You like your relationships with men to be a little more exciting than a friendship with him would be, mm?'

'I like to laugh more often than I think Christopher does. He doesn't appear to have a very active sense of humour.'

'It's no laughing matter, seeing the girl you fancy snaffled by someone else—particularly by a Greek peasant,' he added sardonically.

'Oh, Dion, why should he regard you in that light?'

'Because I think he's inherited a "wogs begin at Calais" mentality.'

She was inclined to agree, but felt obliged to defend Christopher by saying, 'If he felt like that about foreigners, he wouldn't come here for a holiday. He'd go to Bournemouth or Torquay.'

'It rains too much there, and the sea is colder. Coming abroad makes him and his like enjoyably conscious of the innate superiority of the true blue Englishman.'

'You're beginning to sound like a man with a chip on his shoulder!'

Prompted by an indefinable impulse, she linked arms with him, pressing his arm to her side in a gesture of affectionate teasing.

He looked down at her. 'Yes, I suppose I do. In fact it isn't a chip—merely an intense irritation with that kind of chauvinism. I imagine I don't have to tell you that before the term "male chauvinist pig" was invented, the word meant exaggerated patriotism. I believe in loving one's country but, above all, in loving mankind. Nationalism, racialism, even religion—I deplore them all because they set people against each other. What this planet needs——' He stopped short. 'I'm sorry, I'm starting to lecture.'

'You aren't sounding at all like a simple Greek peasant,' she said, smiling.

They were passing through a narrow alley, with lights and people ahead but not where they were at that moment.

Dion checked his stride and bent his head. His mouth pressed warmly on hers in a brief but pulse-quickening kiss.

'I am a man,' he said huskily. 'And you are a beautiful woman. The pleasure we can give each other is all that matters in the long run.'

Some children ran past. They walked on, his arm round her waist, as if they were already lovers. They passed one restaurant, fenced in by head-high chain-link with bunches of grapes hanging down from the vine above the tables. A few yards farther on was Dodo's, half the fore-court tables occupied.

'I'm told that the washrooms here are exceptionally clean, if you want to make use of the women's one,' said Dion.

Wondering who had given him that report, Valissa went off to unplait her hair and give it a vigorous brushing. Having set out that morning with the expectation of returning to Loggos long before this, she had brought nothing with her to give her appearance a lift. But the little mirror above the basin reflected a face glowing with health, and the extra radiance of a girl to whom it has just been demonstrated that she is extremely desirable.

Dion rose as he saw her returning.

'Your informant, whoever she was, was quite right,' she told him, as he drew out a chair for her.

If he recognised her curiosity, he did not indulge it. 'I'm glad to hear it,' was all he said.

The *tavérna* had no written menu, and only one small, black-eyed, energetic waiter whom Valissa took to be Dodo.

'We have beans, stuffed tomatoes, stuffed peppers, shish kebab, pork chop, pizza. . . .' He reeled off the night's bill of fare.

'I'd like to try some *retsina*,' she told Dion, when asked what she would like to drink.

She had heard that it tasted like turpentine, but wanted to make her own judgment.

For their first course, Dion had recommended the beans which turned out to be haricot beans deliciously flavoured with herbs. The pizzas which followed were generous in size, the dough thin and chewy so that it was easier to cut them into sections to eat with the fingers. The *retsina* she liked, finding the flavour of resin far less strong than she had expected.

While they ate, Dion talked about sailboarding, a sea sport still in its infancy in Paxos.

'But in the south of France it's getting to the point where they may have to introduce laws to avoid the accidents which can happen when a beach has too many windsurfers,' he told her. 'No one is more of an enthusiast than I am, but I have to concede it's not right for ordinary bathers to have their pleasure spoilt by the danger of being cracked on the head by a speeding sailboard. Next week, if you like, when your palms are back to normal, I'll give you a lesson.'

His assumption that she had another week's holiday to come was probably because he had not seen her around the previous week. Valissa did not correct his misapprehension. She had already made up her mind that, unless it endangered her job, she *was* going to be here next week. Accommodation was no problem. There was no one else coming to stay in Andrew's apartment. Where she might meet an insuperable difficulty was in getting her flight back to London postponed.

If the worst comes to the worst, I'll have to go back on a scheduled flight, she thought recklessly. I *must* have more time here. It may be crazy, but I must.

Aloud, she said, 'I'd love to have a go, but it looks as if it needs a lot of muscle.'

'On the contrary, it's largely technique. I've seen children as young as seven doing it. Admittedly they need smaller sails, but you have a lot more strength than a seven-year-old.'

He put one hand on her upper arm and, with his other, folded her fingers into a fist and lifted it towards her shoulder.

'For a girl, that's not a bad biceps. You could pack quite a punch if you wanted to. I'd better remember that when I'm seeing you home tonight,' he said quizzically.

'Yes, I might be a black belt or something, for all you know,' she answered lightly.

But she couldn't help remembering Christopher's warning. *Was* she making a fool of herself? Was Dion a sexual opportunist who, when he married, would choose a decorous Greek girl, but until then took full advantage of the more lax morals of foreign girls?

A Paxiot walked past the restaurant, saw Dion among the diners, and raised a hand to him. They looked about the same age and had probably been to school together. Had the other man, noticing her, smiled to himself, thinking—Dionysios won't be sleeping alone tonight.

It was a discomfiting possibility that everyone local, seeing them together, would jump to the same conclusion.

'You're worried about something. What is it?' he asked.

'Worried? Why should I be worried?'

'I don't know, unless you tell me. But your face is very expressive. It isn't a mask, like most faces. I can see when you're shy or amused, or happy. Just now you were troubled, Valissa.'

Seeing that he meant to persist, she fabricated a reason.

'I was wondering how many calories there were in that pizza. You might not think it, seeing me now, but I used to be a very plump teenager, and I don't want to go back to London several pounds heavier than I came.'

'In London you don't swim for hours. That will counterbalance the extra food. I don't like women whose bones show.' He paused. 'But that isn't the reason you were worried. I think perhaps you're afraid of me, because you know I want to make love to you—and because you want it as well. You aren't used to so strong an attraction happening so quickly. If we were in London, and I were an Englishman, it would be less alarming. But you're abroad, I'm a foreigner, and you don't know where you are with me as you have with your other lovers.'

She was about to admit to him that there had been no other lovers, when she realised that the middle-aged couple at the next table had been straining their ears to listen to what Dion was saying, and were now agog for her reply.

'There are people waiting for a table. Shall we let them have ours, and have our coffee in the *platia*?' she suggested.

'By all means.'

By the time he had paid the bill, and they could return to the square, she was having second thoughts about telling him the truth about herself. He had stopped kissing her at the cottage because he had thought her too young for him. He might have similar scruples about seducing a virgin—even one of nearly twenty-four. At the moment she hadn't made up her mind whether she wanted him to be the man to change that for her. But she did know that she didn't want him to lose interest in her.

'The people at the next table were eavesdropping on us. I think the wife was probably envious. Her husband looked rather stolid. I'm sure you could sweep her off her feet with no trouble at all,' she said lightly.

'Are you implying that that is my intention with you?' he asked.

'Isn't it?'

'On the contrary, when I thought you were young and

inexperienced, I deliberately drew back from a situation which was very much to my advantage,' he reminded her. 'Ah, I think I see what concerns you. You suspect I may make a habit of this, is that it? That I'm some kind of ageing beach boy, preying on susceptible female tourists?'

'No, of course I don't think that,' she protested.

'Maybe you didn't think it, but Carter did. You wouldn't have told him you could take care of yourself if he hadn't said something detrimental.'

Valissa didn't answer. They were passing through the dark part of the alley where, earlier on, he had kissed her. This time Dion didn't touch her.

When, at the corner, she would have turned left towards the *platia*, he took her by the elbow.

'You're right: for this kind of conversation it's better to have a little privacy. We'll take a stroll now and have coffee later.'

He steered her towards another alley, a short-cut to the waterfront. There, he turned away from the centre towards the less frequented quays. The few souvenir shops along there were closed by this time of night, but from the windows of the houses light shone on the black-glass surface of the water, undisturbed now by the wash of passing craft.

Because a large island lay within a sling-shot of Gaios, the expanse of water between them always seemed to Valissa more like a bend of a river than a harbour such as the one at Loggos.

Out of nervousness rather than curiosity, she asked, 'What is the name of that island?'

'Agios Nikolaos—Saint Nicholas. It's privately owned. One can only go there with permission. On the seaward side—you can't see it from here—is Panagia or Madonna Island. There's a nunnery on it which was at one time a sanctuary for a silent Order. But the last two nuns to live there both died in 1972. Hardly anyone goes there now except in August when they hold a procession on Our Lady's Day.'

'How does the Greek Orthodox Church differ from other churches?' she asked, again to put off discussing their personal relationship.

'Eastern Orthodox is the correct name. The dogma is much the same as Roman Catholic dogma. The Vatican holds all Eastern churches to be in schism but not in heresy. But there's a good deal of difference in the style of worship—icons instead of images, and no organ music. Also the *pappades*—the priests—are generally married. If they want promotion, they have to divorce their wives who then go to live in a convent,' he added sardonically.

'I don't like the sound of that much. In fact the whole idea of promotion, and high rank, and lavish vestments always seems to me totally incompatible with Christian principles.'

'I agree, but, if you remember, we didn't leave Dodo's in order to discuss spiritual matters,' he replied, with a tinge of mockery.

'Dion . . . please . . . as I told you before, it's too soon,' she said, in a low tone.

'And I said I'd give you more time. But I didn't promise not to kiss you.'

There was no one within a hundred yards. He took her firmly in his arms, one hand in her hair, tilting her head back.

'Don't you want me to kiss you, Valissa?' he murmured, close to her mouth.

Her lips trembled. Deep inside, she felt herself melting with longing, her body clamouring to surrender, only her mind holding back.

Dion kissed her, but only lightly.

'I think I should take you home now. You had a disturbed night last night, and tomorrow we're going to Antipaxos, and in the evening to Mogonisi. Tonight you should go to bed early. Don't worry—alone,' he teased her.

Riding back on the motorbike, she was glad of the jacket he had borrowed for her. Earlier, spinning along the coast road, she had needed only a light hold. But on the way back to her village there were places where the road was steeper, and she had to cling close to his broad back.

The *tavernas* were still serving drinks when they rode down the hill into Loggos. A large, beautiful yacht had put in, and was anchored in the middle of the harbour. Someone on board was playing a guitar. The sound drifted over the water and mingled with the laughing conversation of a party of holidaymakers.

As Valissa dismounted, she expected Dion to follow suit, but instead he remained astride the motorbike.

'I'll come and fetch you about nine. Okay?'

'Yes ... fine. Don't you want any coffee?' she asked, with a glance at the café tables.

'I'll have something to drink when I get home. Goodnight, Valissa. Sleep well.'

He did a U-turn and was gone, leaving her standing in the lamplight, a little disappointed, a little puzzled.

The next morning, before Dion fetched her, she telephoned London and spoke to Elizabeth Barclay.

English Summer Time being two hours behind Greek time, at half past eight in Paxos it would be half past six in London. But Elizabeth was an early riser, never in bed after six o'clock, and with an extension in her bathroom, so Valissa had no fears that calling at an early hour would prejudice her case.

'Is something the matter, Valissa?' the older girl asked, when she learned who was calling.

'No, everything's fine,' Valissa assured her. 'Listen, is Eliot going to blow his top if I'm a week late coming back? Something's come up ... something important. But I don't want to get back to London and find I've been given the sack.'

There was a short silence before Elizabeth replied, '*Cherchez l'homme*, I presume? It can only be a man. Who is he?'

Valissa stifled a laugh. 'He's a Greek, and the whole thing is crazy. But I've only just met him, and now ... well, I can't leave just yet.'

'I should think not indeed,' said Elizabeth. 'You stay there, my dear. I'll fix Eliot. I couldn't be more delighted that at last you've met someone special. I've been worried about you ... yes, really. It isn't natural for a girl as attractive as you are to be totally immersed in her work.'

'I don't know that he is special. But he may be. I want to find out.'

'You do that. Don't worry about a thing. I'll tell Eliot you've picked up a bug, and the doctor won't let you travel.'

They talked for a few more minutes, and then Valissa rang off, relieved and amused by Elizabeth's forthright approval.

The night before, she had tried on the bark-pleated dress and found it was much more transparent than she had realised in the shop. Her white micro-briefs showed through the thin blue cheesecloth, but luckily she had brought one tan-coloured pair with her. In these she appeared to be naked, and indeed this was true of her top half as the loose style made a bra unnecessary for someone with small, firm breasts. That it could be a folly she might regret to go disco-dancing with Dion in a filmy dress and little else was a thought she pushed out of her mind. She had no other clothes which were suitable.

At two or three minutes to nine, there was a rat-tat on her door. She opened it to find him smiling at her, morning-spruce in a clean shirt and shorts, with his lean jaw smoothly shaven, and his thick curls as glossy as a bird's wing. As he ducked to avoid hitting the lintel, she caught the faint, pleasant scent of either his shampoo or aftershave.

'This is very attractive. Your work?' he asked, looking round the spacious room.

Valissa shook her head. She explained about Andrew and Susan.

'They both have excellent taste. But even someone who hasn't can hardly go wrong if they shop at Laura Ashley and Habitat. If I had sufficient money to set up in business on my own, that's the market I'd like to compete in. One-off designing for the very rich doesn't appeal to me as much as making it possible for ordinary people, on tight budgets, to have homes which are equally stylish.'

Dion was strolling round the room, studying it. 'Do you know how the profits compare? Who makes more money? Your boss, or these two firms you've mentioned?'

'Hard to say. In America, Eliot charges two thousand dollars an hour for a private consultation. But in that amount of time he could design an object for the mass market which might make two thousand seem like peanuts.' On the point of expanding this statement, she changed her mind. 'I mustn't start talking shop. It's only interesting to people in the same line.'

'The ways other people make money is never uninteresting to me.'

'Do you want to make money, Dion? When you called yourself a jack-of-all-trades, you sounded as if you were happy to make just enough to keep the wolf from the door.'

He shrugged. 'There are times when I'm content with a simple life, and times when I want more,' he answered. He came towards her. 'Today I have two thousand drachs in my pocket, the most beautiful girl on the island as my companion, and nothing to do but enjoy myself. Would it make *you* any happier if, instead of riding to Gaios on the back of Alessandro's old bike, I had an expensive car outside, and a sixty-metre yacht in the harbour?'

'If you had, you wouldn't be you. You'd be older, maybe several times married, and probably soft with rich living. And one has a better view of the scenery from the back of a bike,' she answered laughingly.

Then minutes later, sitting behind him, breathing in the fresh woodland scents of cypress and bracken and wild herbs, she knew that no millionaire's girl-friend, cruising the Ionian Sea in luxury, could possibly be happier than she was on this hot, glorious morning, with her knees gripping Dion's flanks, and her hands on his wide, strong shoulders.

The caique taking people to Antipaxos was already crowded when they arrived. But they found a place to stand on the narrow stretch of deck by the wheel-house, and from there they had an excellent view of the south-east coast of Paxos from the sea.

Presently the caique turned through a narrow channel between Mogonisi Island and the islet of Kalkionisi, on which stood a small, lonely chapel dedicated to Saint Spyridon.

'In life, he was a bishop,' said Dion, in answer to her enquiry about the saint. 'He's supposed to have saved the town of Corfu from the Turks, from a famine, and twice from the plague. At Easter, and again in November, they carry his mummified body round the town in a glass-fronted palanquin, with a band and all the civic dignitaries walking ahead. For a long time the mummy was private property, and a family named Voulgaris made a very good thing from it. But about fifty years ago he was taken over by the government. No end of male children are called after him. If you were to shout "Spiro!" in any of the village squares there, at least a dozen men would think you were calling them.'

Within half an hour of leaving Gaios they were close to the strange folded rock formations of the cliffs of Antipaxos. Soon their destination was in sight, a crescent of smooth pale sand lapped by water which, where it was deeper, was as blue as the sky overhead.

The caique was moored to a concrete jetty some way from the beach which the passengers reached by climbing over the rocks at the foot of the cliff. A similar cliff rose from the other end of the bay, and behind the beach the ground sloped gradually upwards to a distant ridge.

Unlike the island they had left, Antipaxos had few olive trees and was given over to vineyards. Not long after their arrival, an old man came down to sell white grapes to the tourists. Dion bought a large bunch which he washed in the sea. Their juicy sweetness, slightly salted, was a flavour Valissa felt she would remember for ever.

More than once, in the six hours they spent there, Dion helped her to re-apply sun cream.

'You aren't in favour of monokinis, I gather,' he said, while she was sitting cross-legged, and he was spreading cream over her shoulder-blades.

His remark had been prompted by two girls walking past without tops on.

'Not for myself. I don't mind them on other people. I suppose, from a man's point of view, it makes sitting on the beach more interesting.'

'It does for those two old boys,' he said dryly, indicating the grape-seller and another old man, now sitting in the shade of a branch-built beach hut, both eyeing with rapt interest the semi-nude bodies all around them.

'At fifteen or sixteen I should have shared their enthusiasm, but now I find an element of mystery more
interesting. Not that much is hidden by a bikini, but it
does allow one to exercise a little imagination—which is
often better than the reality,' he added.

Valissa twisted to look at him. 'That sounds very disillusioned.'

He smiled at her. She had discovered that the strange,
changeable colour of his eyes was because, in the same
way that hazel eyes were basically green flecked with
brown, his irises were grey flecked with gold.

'I don't think I shall be disillusioned when I undress
you, Valissa.'

She felt herself starting to blush and turned back to
look at the sea. He was sure they were going to be lovers.
If she didn't feel the same way, why had she telephoned
Elizabeth and organised another week's holiday?

From behind her, he said, 'I like it—your shyness, your
modesty. Boldness isn't becoming in a woman. The girl
who flaunts her body on the beach isn't necessarily as
uninhibited in bed.' His voice deepened. 'I've already had
proof of how warm and responsive you can be.'

She felt his lips brush her shoulder, and a long thrilling
shudder ran through her.

I'm in love with him, she thought, startled. But how
can I be? In two days? He's a stranger. I hardly know
him.

CHAPTER FOUR

THERE had not been time to return the borrowed blue jacket before the trip to Antipaxos. When, about half past four, they disembarked from the ferry, Valissa said, 'Does your friend like chocolates, do you know? I want to give her a small present for her kindness in lending me her jacket.'

'She said you were welcome to keep it for the rest of your stay. It's one she no longer wears. It's too small for her now.'

'I've brought a wrap of my own to wear tonight,' she explained.

Having bought some sweets, she went with Dion to thank Maria in person. It seemed there were as many Marias on Paxos as there were Spiros in Corfu.

This Maria looked several years older than Dion, probably because, although her legs were slim, she was considerably overweight, and was obviously wearing old-fashioned and ageing foundation garments under her matronly sun-dress.

Traces of youthful prettiness still remained. She had noticeably long eyelashes, and a small nose and sweetly-curved mouth. But if she had once been a belle, she had long since surrendered that claim and was now devoting herself to being an exemplary housewife and mother. The interior of her home was immaculate, and her toddler and baby were clearly the light of her life.

She was delighted with the sweets, and insisted that her visitors must stay to have coffee and spoonfuls of fruit preserve. This Valissa found rather sickly, although she took care not to show it. Even in her own plump phase she had never had a very sweet tooth, but clearly Maria loved sugary things and saw no reason to deny herself.

Perhaps she did not even realise there was a connection between her appetite and her weight. Judging by her conversation—interpreted by Dion because she spoke no

English—she was a warmhearted woman but not an intelligent one.

The visit made Valissa conscious that Dion's female relations were probably very much like Maria; and that Maria's complete preoccupation with her home and children and, presumably, with the comfort of her fisherman husband, was something Dion would expect when he came to marry.

Once Valissa had felt that she, too, would be totally content to be Nick's wife. Now she wasn't so sure that marriage would completely fulfil her; certainly not the kind of unrelieved domesticity which this Maria, and the one at Loggos, and Anna, seemed to accept as their natural rôle in life.

Why am I thinking about marriage? she asked herself, as she walked with Dion back to the square to await the next boat to Mogonisi.

She knew it was because she was dangerously close to falling in love with him and, for her, love and marriage were concomitant. It might be old-fashioned thinking in an era when many of her contemporaries seemed to see marriage as a commitment they were unwilling to take on now there was no longer any stigma attached to living together.

But, old-fashioned or not, it was how she felt. Perhaps being brought up by an elderly couple, who were still each other's dearest person after nearly half a century of marriage, had a good deal to do with her attitude.

Her grandparents had been living proof that "happy ever after" was not merely wishful thinking. It happened. She felt sure it would have happened to her, if Nick had lived. It might yet happen.

But not with Dion. He was nowhere near loving her. She was just a bedworthy foreign girl whom he hoped to add to his conquests. Of whom, no doubt, there had been many.

The ferry to Mogonisi was smaller than the one to Antipaxos, with an awning, and a carpet in the well of the boat which was surrounded by benches to seat about twenty-five people, with more space in the bows and on top of the engine housing. However, at this time of day they were the only people wanting to go to Mogonisi. It was late to be going there to swim, and early to be going over for dinner.

The beach at Mogonisi had been invisible when they had passed the island on their way to Antipaxos that morning. It was hidden away round a corner. Behind it was the bar and restaurant to which they were going. There was a rival establishment at one end of the beach, and that also ran a ferry service to and from Gaios. It was customary to patronise the restaurant belonging to the owners of whichever ferry one had travelled on.

'Another swim while the sun lasts?' Dion suggested, when they arrived.

'I think I'll just sunbathe,' said Valissa.

By this time of day, although it was still blissfully warm, it was no longer necessary for her to put on protective cream. Indeed, after almost a fortnight of sensible skin care, she had now achieved a satisfactory tan without either burning or peeling.

She lay on her towel, facing the water. With her chin resting on cupped palms, she watched Dion swim across the inlet to the pinewoods on the far shore.

It was hard to accept how short a time they had known each other. She knew she must make up her mind whether or not to have a brief, heady, heartbreaking love affair with him. But although she had already committed herself to the extent of taking an extra week's holiday, she could still draw back from total involvement.

Were a few days and nights of ecstasy worth the loss of her self-respect? For she knew that to take as a lover a man who would never say 'I love you' would be bound to damage her self-esteem.

The decision was made more complex by the fact of her inexperience. The first time was always momentous. While she had no fear that Dion would be insensitive or selfish—he had shown in a dozen small ways that he was considerate and chivalrous—would his experience and skill compensate for his lack of deep feeling?

Ideally, she would have liked to have had a shower and to shampoo her hair again before putting on the blue dress. But as she had to change in the women's washroom, the best she could do was to give her hair a vigorous brushing, apply some eye make-up, and spray herself lavishly with the atomiser of *l'Air du Temps* she had bought on the plane.

When she emerged to join Dion at the bar, she found that he had changed into a pair of clean jeans and a dark red tee-shirt. He had also had a shave, she noticed. His jaw, beginning to darken when he had come out of the water, was now as smooth as it had been first thing that morning.

With the unfailing good manners which either were instinctive with him, or which he had acquired by closely observing the behaviour of sophisticated people, he rose from his stool as soon as he saw her coming.

'Is that the dress you bought yesterday?' he asked, following his first swift appraisal with a second slower scrutiny.

'Yes; it really needs sandals to match, but these are not too bad,' she said, glancing down at her holiday shoes which were an adaptation of a French espadrille with medium high rope-covered wedges and long tapes criss-crossed round her slender ankles. They were mimosa yellow, the accent colour she had chosen to go with mainly white holiday separates.

'I like them. You have pretty ankles. And a beautiful body of which, when you came down the steps, that dress gave some very enticing glimpses. You're going to attract a lot of attention when the dancing begins later on,' he told her.

'I hope not,' said Valissa, dismayed. Was the dress as diaphanous as that?

The dance floor was a circle of concrete, with a roof suspended above it by ropes slung over the branches of the surrounding olive trees. At present it was lit by fairy lights, but later the disco light would be switched on and she had no wish to become a cynosure because of a too see-through dress.

Dion looked amused. 'Don't you like to be admired?'

'I shouldn't like to feel I was being leered at. Do I . . . do I look very naked?'

'For me, not naked enough. I should like to see you

dressed like Aphrodite,' he teased her. 'But no, to be serious, you are not showing anything which can't be seen in your bikini. Somehow the effect, through the dress, is more erotic, that's all. But if I catch anyone leering at you, he won't do it twice,' he added, with a touch of crispness which suggested that he wasn't speaking idly.

They sat under the trees, drinking wine. It was night now. On the hillside across the water, the lights of two or three isolated houses were golden pinpoints in the darkness. The water was still, except when the wake of a boat caused a few gentle ripples to come lapping over the deserted strand. The busy world and all its troubles seemed far, far away from this peaceful place.

'Are you happy?' Dion asked her suddenly.

Valissa considered the question.

Certainly it was some time since she had stopped being actively unhappy. But although, in the past two years, her capacity to enjoy a spring morning, a delicious meal, a Christmas Day spent with her grandfather, had revived, she had never recovered the abounding joy in being alive which she had experienced in Nick's time.

Perhaps it had had something to do with being nineteen years old, as well as being in love. Or perhaps, if she abandoned herself to a love affair with Dion, she would recapture it—for a short time.

'Who wouldn't be?' she answered lightly. 'I've had a lovely day. I'm enjoying sitting here, drinking this wine and talking to you. I'm looking forward to my supper. Who wouldn't be happy in these circumstances?'

Perhaps two glasses of wine had loosened her tongue, as she didn't let it go at that, but went on, 'Only I can remember being happy on a wet winter night in London, waiting for a bus which was half an hour late. My shoes were soaked and I was cold, but I was happy in spite of it. So how does one define happiness?'

'You were with your young man, presumably?' Dion said quietly.

'Yes, and he was full of wonderful, star-reaching ambitions which I was going to share with him. We were so certain about everything. Certain Nick was going to be famous. Certain we should have enough money for a large old house in the country filled with books and paintings, and all the other things we both liked. Certain we should have at least two children. Did you feel like that at nineteen, Dion? Were you sure, then, of making your fortune, and marrying a beautiful girl, and always being happy and successful?'

'I felt I should make my fortune—yes. I don't recall marriage being high on my list of priorities. There are exceptions, of course, but the majority of young men are interested in amorous adventures rather than in marriage,' was his dry reply.

'Also the Greeks take a more practical view of marriage than the English and the Americans,' he went on. 'A more serious view, you could say. A Greek doesn't start married life with the feeling that, if it doesn't work out, he can call it quits and try again. He expects his marriage to last, and for that it must be based on a stronger foundation than romantic love.'

'Does a Greek discount romantic love altogether?'

'In general—yes.'

'And what is your personal view? When or if you eventually marry, will it be for sensible reasons?'

'I'm not a typical Greek. Having travelled and spent a great part of my life among non-Greeks, I've been influenced by their attitudes. Now, unfortunately, I shall only be satisfied with a woman who combines the old-fashioned virtues of the Paxiot wife with the attractions of a girl like yourself, and finding one could be an impossible quest.'

'Looking at it from her point of view, are you offering the old-fashioned virtues of a Paxiot husband in addition to your attractions?'

At this point their conversation was interrupted by the high-pitched hooting of the ferry, bringing a full load of passengers.

Instead of answering her question, Dion said, 'It looks as if the crews of the flotilla are about to descend on us. It might be a good idea to go and choose a table before they arrive.'

His hand rested lightly on the back of her waist as they went up the flights of stone steps which connected the terrace of the restaurant with the bar and dance floor on the lower level. Dion chose a table with an uninterrupted view of the bay below, and a waiter had taken their order before the crowd of newcomers were all ashore.

As her companion showed no inclination to resume the subject they had been discussing a few minutes earlier, Valissa did not return to it. Soon bowls of peppery bean soup had been set before them, with a basket of bread and bottles of water and wine.

While they were waiting for their next course to be served, the flotilla people began to come up to the restaurant, whereupon all the unoccupied tables were arranged to form two large open-ended rectangles. The purpose of this was not made clear until later when, towards the end of their meal, one of the liveliest members of the sailing crowd became a self-appointed master of ceremonies and started community singing.

By this time Valissa and Dion were having coffee. She wondered how he would react. His English was so idiomatic that he would understand the words as well as she did, and might enjoy joining in, as the diners not with the flotilla were being encouraged to by the ebullient M.C.

For her own part, Valissa would have preferred to take part in some form of Greek entertainment rather than this typically English activity which, not being an uninhibited extrovert, she did not really enjoy.

However, when Dion added a pleasant baritone to the chorus of voices roaring *Oh, my darling Clementine*, she joined in with a good grace, but hoping the flotilla people were not going to impose their corporate personality on the whole of the rest of the evening.

Presently, as she was rather hypocritically applauding a member of the group who had performed a comic solo, Dion leaned towards her.

'Shall we go down?'

She nodded. Before someone else began their party piece, they left their table and slipped away.

'A lively lot, aren't they?' he said, as they went down the steps. 'Mostly North Country people and Midlanders, by the sound of it. More like rugby players than most of the yachtsmen I've encountered. I wonder what happens if a quiet pair of southerners find themselves allocated to share with a couple of non-stop comedians?'

'I was wondering about that myself. But I shouldn't
think people who weren't good mixers would choose that
kind of holiday.'

'I consider I'm a good mixer, but one can have too
much conviviality,' said Dion, as a rousing rendering of
On Ilkla Moor Baht 'At broke out on the upper terrace.

However, it did not drown the music being played
below, and a few moments later they were dancing.

It was years since she had been on a dance floor, but at
one time she had loved to dance. Now, with none of the
reluctance she had felt about joining in the singing, she
surrendered to the pulsing rhythm.

Much later, the two young Greeks who ran the place
gave a demonstration of folk dancing, their arms round
each other's shoulders, their feet following a pattern which
seemed to Valissa never to repeat itself.

At first the music was slow. As the tempo began to
increase, they were joined by the skipper of the flotilla
who had probably mastered the steps during several sum-
mers in the Ionian.

'Do you mind if I leave you?' Dion asked her.

'Of course not.'

Smiling, she watched him run forward to join the other
three.

From then on he was the only one she had eyes for as
the pace grew steadily faster, and the four men circled the
floor, performing the intricate movements with increasing
swiftness and vigour.

She had read that the finest dancers were usually
fishermen and workmen, dancing for their own pleasure.
Certainly the dance she was watching would have over-
taxed the strength of a white collar worker, unless he was
unusually fit.

Feet flying, powerful thighs flexing as, swooping and
leaping, he matched the steps of the others, Dion flashed
a grin in her direction. Clearly he was enjoying himself.
Equally clearly she realised that from now on, whenever
she heard the twanging notes of a *bouzoukia*, she would see
a mental picture of him; this dark, virile man of Paxos to
whom, with each hour that passed, she was in greater

danger of losing her heart.

'That was wonderful, Dion!' she told him, when he returned to her.

He laughed. 'It's good exercise.'

But strenuous as the dance had been, he wasn't breathing any faster than after dancing with her.

She thought of her male colleagues in London with their soft hands and flabby bodies, pale-skinned as her own had been before her two weeks in the sun. Compared with them, he was a god.

What if he had none of their assets; no money, no profession, no social standing, only his grandparents' cottage and a rubber dinghy with an outboard?

'They're starting again. Come and try it.' He seized her by the wrist, pulling her with him to the dance floor where others beside herself were going to attempt the folk dance.

Soon a line of a dozen or more people were trying to emulate the practised steps of the four men strung out among them.

'Very good,' said Dion in her ear as, watching his feet, she did her best to improve on the rather clumsy performance of the giggling girl on the other side of him.

By the time it was over she was breathless. As the line broke up and dispersed, he put both arms round her and held her loosely against him while she recovered her breath.

The bright pink lights dimmed, giving place to a dim purple glow which made white clothing look fluorescent. Some new music began, not *bouzoukia* but a pop group playing a slow number.

Drawing Valissa closer, Dion began a night club shuffle.

'Put your arms round my neck,' he murmured.

After some seconds' hesitation, Valissa slid her hands up his arms and locked them behind his strong neck, letting herself relax completely, wondering if it was folly to let him mould her body to his in this intimate fashion. Other people were dancing in the same way, but some of them were married, and those who were not had known each other for much longer than she and Dion, of that she felt positive.

About two o'clock in the morning she found herself in the same posture but in different circumstances.

Now they were alone in the moonlit lane outside the door of her apartment, and he was not merely holding her but kissing her.

When, a few minutes later, it turned out that he had been kissing her goodnight, she was taken aback, having thought that he was weakening her resistance to letting him spend the rest of the night with her.

'I won't collect you so early tomorrow. You'll want to sleep later,' he said, in a low tone, when he released her. 'Say about half past ten. Is that okay?'

'That's fine. Thank you for today.'

The cost of it must have made a sizeable hole in his two thousand drachmas. He had paid for everything, firmly rejecting her attempts to contribute to their expenses.

'My pleasure. Goodnight.' And he left her.

The next day, before he came for her, Valissa made some more telephone calls and was able to rearrange her flight home. Dion fetched her by boat—the motorbike being back with its owner—and gave her a lesson in sailboarding.

Getting up on the board wasn't too difficult. Even raising the sail she could master, once he had shown her the way of it. But keeping the mast up, and catching the wind in the sail, was another matter.

He had managed to borrow a board in addition to the one which was his. While she was practising, and falling off at frequent intervals, he was skimming back and forth with the expertise of an experienced windsurfer.

He would not let her try again after lunch.

'If you overdo it the first day, you'll be all aches and pains tomorrow. Pity about that bruise on your thigh.'

They were standing near the water's edge, and suddenly he went down on his haunches and, grasping her leg with both hands, pressed his mouth softly on the place where a knock from the board was already beginning to show itself.

Valissa drew in a sharp breath which became an incoherent murmur as, equally suddenly, he straightened, and transferred his mouth to hers.

'You don't need any lessons in kissing,' he murmured, a little while later. 'There's no one about. Do you really need all these clothes on?'—his fingers going to the strings at the nape of her neck.

'Oh, Dion, please . . . no . . . not here! There's a boat going past,' she protested, pulling away.

The brief bathing trunks he was wearing left no doubt of his urgent desire, and his eyes were fierce and devouring as he scanned the soft contours exposed by her own scanty coverings.

Valissa sensed that it was in his mind to swing her up into his arms, as he had the night he had rescued her, and carry her into the shade of a grove of pine trees behind the beach. There the ground had a carpet of dried needles, and the shade made it relatively private.

For a moment she knew herself to be helpless, not only against his superior strength, but against her own trembling longing to be made a woman by this tough, tender, exciting Greek.

'No, you're right . . . not here,' he said thickly.

An instant later she watched him plunge into the sea, and knew herself safe and unscathed, at least for the time being. But whether she was glad or sorry, she could not tell.

They dined on the waterfront at Loggos, and again he kissed her goodnight at her door, but without attempting to come inside.

Perhaps he knew that with each embrace her resistance weakened. Perhaps he hoped that tomorrow night she would be at a pitch to invite him in. After that, whatever happened, she would never be able to accuse him of overwhelming her, because it would be she herself who had taken the crucial initiative.

Valissa didn't like to believe that this was the way his mind worked. On the other hand, he must have some reason, some strategy for delaying his ultimate conquest of her.

It could be that he was a man who, however strong his

desire, never took a woman unless he was sure she was willing; and who knew that Valissa still had doubts.

These, and many other suppositions, kept her awake for a long time after he had left her. There were moments during that restless night when she wished she had never set eyes on him; and other moments when she knew that only because she *had* met him had the ghost of her young love, her first love, at last ceased to haunt her.

None of her night thoughts came anywhere near the actual way in which Dion brought their relationship to its climax.

The next day—the day she should have been back at her desk in London—they spent the morning sailboarding, after which they returned to the village to have a light lunch on her roof terrace.

Afterwards, they were going to swim from the nearby beach and then, in the cooler temperature of late afternoon, walk to Lakka and have supper there.

It was a particularly hot day, but the roof terrace caught such little breeze as there was, and in the green shade of the vine they drank chilled white wine and ate a salad which she had prepared after breakfast and left in the refrigerator.

Dion was surprisingly knowledgeable about the history of the Ionion islands. He told her how, in the sixteenth and seventeenth centuries, Zakinthos and Cefalonia, the two larger islands south of Paxos, had become rich by trading in currants. The English had been particularly good customers, although what they did with their purchases had been a mystery to the islanders who knew nothing of plum cakes and puddings.

Valissa was still asking him questions when they cleared the table and washed up.

'I'll get our things off the line,' she said, meaning the beach towels and bathing kit they had pegged out to dry before eating.

Dion did not reply. He had picked up one of her books and was reading the blurb on the wrapper.

By the time she returned to the living-room he had put down the book and was standing in the centre of the room, waiting for her to hand him his things—or so she thought.

But as he took them from her, he said, 'We can swim later on. Right now I think it's high time we reached what an English poet called "the right true end of love".'

By the time she realised what he meant, she was in his arms, being kissed with the unmistakable authority of a man who, this time, was not going to be content with anything less than her total surrender.

So, at last, this is it, she thought dizzily as, by swaying her backwards, Dion made her let go of the towels and cling to his powerful shoulders. As his hard body closed with her soft one, his kiss grew fiercer; no longer coaxing a response from her, but exacting it, forcing her submission.

The first kiss seemed to go on for ever, drowning her in a whirlpool of sensuality. She was conscious of nothing but the shivers of delight along her nerves, the pounding of her heart and pulses, the ache of longing deep inside her.

That he gave her no chance to protest when he carried her to the bed disguised as a couch was, at that moment, what she wanted. A primeval desire to be mastered made her glad that he sealed her lips with another long kiss which did not end until she was lying among the cushions and he was stretched out beside her.

All the time he was kissing her eyelids, she knew he was unfastening the shirt which, with shorts, was her only covering. Seconds later he was touching her breasts, sending renewed shudders through her as his warm hand caressed the soft flesh which, hidden from the sun, was still ivory pale.

'They're beautiful,' he said softly. 'Everything about you is beautiful, my lovely girl.'

Her eyes closed, Valissa smiled. Her fingers were in his dark hair, enjoying the crisp springy curls which clustered so thickly on his skull.

He was beautiful, too, she thought hazily, as his hand went on gently stroking and his mouth taught her ways of kissing which, in four years, she had half forgotten, and some which she had never learned.

For a long time he seemed content to continue this leisurely love-play; or, if not content, prepared to delay the fierce passion she had felt burning in him at first.

He couldn't possibly know how long it was since she had given her lips to anyone willingly. Nor would it cross his mind that a girl of her age might never have made love before.

Yet, if he had known both those facts, he couldn't have done more to make the experience as pleasurable as possible for her. Later she thought that, in some ways, it would have been better if he had been a less practised lover.

Dion stopped kissing her mouth, and his lips traced a path down her throat, lingering over the hollow at its base, then exploring the curves of her shoulders before moving down to her breasts. Instinctively, her spine arched and a soft gasp of pleasure broke from her.

Now his hand was covering her navel ... now unfastening the clip of her shorts ... now drawing down the tag of the zip. When it slipped through the opening she shuddered, but she didn't resist as his palm passed over her belly to the smooth sweep of hip and thigh.

It was not until some seconds later that she began to struggle; a deep-seated instinct resisting the caresses which threatened to rob her of the little control she still had.

'Sshh ... lie still ... relax,' Dion murmured.

He brought his mouth back to hers for a kiss which almost subdued her.

But then a soft tug on her shorts rekindled the fear she had felt; the age-old fear of the girl who knows she is being swept off her feet; and, in her case, the added dread of being added to a long line of easy conquests by a man who would forget her the day she flew home.

Wrenching her mouth free, she began to resist him more strenuously.

'*Khristos!* This is crazy, Valissa. You don't think I'm going to stop now?' He sounded more incredulous than angry.

'You must ... please ... please, Dion ... *I beg you*!'

'No, I'm damned if I will,' he said thickly. 'What are you afraid of? I'm not going to hurt you, silly girl.' His mouth took possession of hers again.

He was so much more powerful than she, that she knew she had no chance against him if he chose to exert any strength. Part of her wished that he would. Part of her wanted to be conquered. But that was her primitive self, the cave-woman in her responding to male domination and her own long-repressed sexuality which he had so skilfully aroused.

Her modern, intelligent self was disgusted by these servile reactions, and made her strain wildly to free herself.

When she started to fight him in earnest, Dion at once let her go. He sprang up, his face strained and angry.

'Don't panic. I'm not going to force you—but that's what will happen to you one day if you make a habit of doing this.'

He turned to stand with his back to her, pounding one fist into the palm of the other hand, every line of his muscular back conveying his fury and frustration.

'I . . . I wasn't teasing you . . . honestly,' she said, in a low, anguished voice. 'At first, when you kissed me . . . I thought . . . but then I knew that I couldn't. I'm sorry . . . I'm truly sorry.'

For a long time he didn't answer, or turn, or do anything but stand there, his deep breathing slowly subsiding.

At last he turned round to face her, his expression no longer as furious, but still rather grim about the mouth.

'I want you, and you want me. We're both grown-up, unmarried people. Explain to me—clearly this time, please—why we can't make love to each other,' he said, in a cool, measured tone.

Valissa was sitting up now, her shorts fastened, her shirt drawn together and buttoned. But everywhere on her body where his lips or his fingers had lingered she felt a special sensitivity, as if her nerve ends were closer to the surface than before.

'Wanting isn't loving,' she answered, avoiding his eyes. 'You said it was time we reached "the right true end of love". If we did love each other, I would let you make love to me. But we don't, and I can't. It's my fault. I should have realised that, with my peculiar ideas, it was unfair to go on seeing you. For me to enjoy making love, I have to be deeply committed. If not I feel . . . cheap and promiscuous.'

'I see.'

She flickered a glance at his set face. Did he see? Did it make any sense to him?

'In that case I hope you won't mind if I ask to be excused from our plan to go over to Lakka?'

'No . . . of course not,' she answered hollowly. Her throat tight with tears, she added, 'Perhaps we'd better say goodbye.'

'I think that's a little premature if you're here for the rest of the week. Paxos is a very small island,' was his clipped response. 'Let's say merely Adieu, shall we?'

She watched him pick up his towel and the black bathing trunks from where they had fallen on the floor when first he embraced her.

A moment later he had gone.

The next morning her pillow was damp from the tears she had wept in the night. She felt tired and profoundly miserable. She felt sure she would never see Dion again, and that her life would revert to what it had been before she met him—an emotional vacuum.

Twice she went to the beach for a swim. The rest of the day she spent moping in the apartment, longing for him to come back. If he had, she would have fallen into his arms. It seemed to her now that to turn down the bliss he had offered her, for the sake of an out-of-date principle, had been an act of insanity.

But the hours dragged, and he didn't come. Why should he?

That night it was stiflingly close. She lay on her bed, naked, unable to sleep for the heat and her memory of him lying beside her.

On the next day they had talked of going to Parga. Unable to endure another long day of her own company, she decided to go on the trip to the mainland by herself.

When the Lakka-based taxi brought her to the *platia* in Gaios, the first person she saw was Dion.

'Good morning,' she greeted him awkwardly.

'Hello, Valissa. Off to Parga?'

She nodded.

'Enjoy yourself.' With a nod, he strolled off towards the kiosk.

Depressed by his indifferent manner, she boarded the caique and found somewhere to sit. She seemed to be the only solitary passenger; all the others were in pairs or groups. She wondered why Dion was in Gaios, but refused to succumb to the temptation of trying to catch another glimpse of him.

She had brought a whodunnit with her, and she began to read it; having to concentrate hard for the first few pages, and then gradually becoming absorbed.

The caique was outside the harbour but still in the lee of the islands of St. Nicholas and Panagia when, out of the corner of her eye, she became aware of a pair of blue-jeaned thighs. For an instant she thought it was the boat-man, coming round to collect the fares. But he was a small man, and the legs belonged to a tall one. She looked up and found Dion watching her.

'I missed you yesterday,' he told her.

'I missed you, too,' she admitted tremulously.

'May I sit down?'—indicating the space occupied by her beach bag and that of the woman next to her.

Valissa moved her bag to the deck, as did the other woman who had noticed Dion's arrival and heard his question.

Smiling his thanks to her, he sat down between them. In a tone which would not be overheard, he said, 'I'm sorry I was angry with you the other day.'

'I deserved it. I'm sorry I gave you cause to be angry with me.'

'Friends again?' he asked, a smile beginning to tilt the corner of his mouth.

'Of course.'

'Good.' He shifted to slip one arm round her shoulders and hug her against him for a moment. Then his arm slackened, but he did not remove it. 'Go on with your book,' he instructed.

It was as well she was wearing her sun-glasses. They concealed the rush of happy tears from the people who were sitting facing them on the coach roof of what, glimpsed through its deck light, appeared to be a disused red plush saloon.

She bent her head, pretending to read, but really

blinking back the tears and savouring the joy of being in
the shelter of his arm.

Five minutes later she closed her book.

'I can't concentrate now,' she murmured, with a smiling upwards glance.

The arm round her tightened again. Speaking close to her
ear, Dion said, 'I was hanging about the quay hoping to see
you. If you hadn't come, I would have come looking for you.'

'Why didn't you come on board with me? To punish
me for a little longer?'

'No, there was something I had to do. It didn't occur
to me till I saw you, and by then there wasn't much time
left if I was going to catch the boat.'

Something in his voice made her look up in time to see
an odd, enigmatic expression on his darkly tanned face.

'What did you have to do?' she asked.

'Just an errand,' he answered evasively. 'You brought
your bathing things, I hope. By the time we've climbed to
the top of the town, we shall want to cool off in the sea.'

Suspecting that his errand had been to buy her some
small peace-offering, Valissa asked no more questions. She
wondered what it might be. She couldn't help wondering
what sort of taste Dion had.

Since he almost always wore tee-shirts and jeans, the
international casual-wear uniform of all kinds of people
from princes and presidents to drop-outs and the very
poor, it was difficult to guess what his formal clothes would
be like—if indeed he possessed any. But with all those
relations he had mentioned, surely he must own a Sunday
best suit for weddings, christenings and funerals?

With his fine physique even an off-the-peg suit, if of good
cloth and cut, would look well on him. In an English bespoke
suit, he would look extremely distinguished. But the probab-
ility was that if he owned a suit it had been made by a small-
town tailor with too much padding in the shoulders and too
much curve at the waist. Then how did he look?

During trips to Spain, France and Italy, on several
occasions she had seen powerfully-built men who would
look magnificent in rough working clothes transformed
into figures of fun by their special occasion clothes. It was
the same when a middle-aged woman dressed like a teen-

ager and made herself look ridiculous and pathetic.

Pushing these uncomfortable thoughts to the back of her mind, Valissa gave herself up to the pleasures of the moment; the gentle motion of the caique as it ploughed across the calm sea, the salty tang of the breeze and, best of all, the relief of being on good terms with Dion, and having his arm round her.

The crossing took almost an hour and a half, although to her it seemed less.

Backed by the towering mountains of Epirus, the fourteenth-century town of Parga straddled the hillside behind a wooded promontory with the ruins of a Venetian fortress on its summit. To the north of this was a sweeping bay, to the south the newer part of the town with the harbour and, beyond it, another bathing beach overlooking several rocky islets.

The waterfront had many cafés, and Dion suggested they should refresh themselves before looking round. Other people made straight for the shops, of which there were a great many more than in Gaios.

'Something very strange happened here at the beginning of the last century,' he told her, while they were drinking wine in the shade of an awning. 'In 1819 the British ceded the town to Ali, the Pasha of Epirus, but the inhabitants didn't want to come under his rule. It was a unanimous decision. On Good Friday, they disinterred the bones of their forebears, burnt them, and took the ashes and their holy icons to Corfu. When the Pasha's troops entered the town, the fires were still smouldering, but there was no one here. So he settled the place with Mohammedans who were here until 1924 when there was a population exchange and they went back to Turkey.'

Valissa said, 'Greece has an incredibly complicated history, hasn't it? Did you learn all that at school?'

'A little of it. Most of it I learned later. Shall we start exploring?'

Although Parga was rather touristy close to the harbour, the steep streets at the back of the town were delightful. Passing a bakery, Dion had stopped to buy rolls still warm from the oven. Eating these, they climbed slowly upwards between the old whitewashed houses with

fading green-painted shutters. Purple bougainvillaea and
pink geraniums cascading over courtyard walls suggested
that Parga had less of a water problem than Paxos.
Wrought iron gates gave glimpses of bushes bright with
the crimson flowers of the hibiscus. Here and there old
men and women sat on the shady side of the street, greet-
ing passers-by with a friendly '*Kalimera*.'

Had the trip allowed them more time, they would have
descended the hill to the northern bay. But the boat
returned to the island at half past two, and it seemed a
better use of the few hours there to retrace their steps and
swim from the southern beach.

After the fairly stiff climb with the heat of mid-morning
beating back from the white walls, it was heavenly to slip
into the clear, cool water and strike out for the nearest of
the islets.

When they waded ashore on the little beach, Dion
asked, 'What did you do with yourself yesterday?'

'Nothing much. I felt too depressed by our quarrel,'
Valissa said candidly. 'I'm not one of those people who
seem to thrive on rows and emotional scenes. I felt very
badly about having led you on and then . . . backed off.'

Was she being too frank with him? she wondered.
Would it have been wiser to ignore what had happened
the day before yesterday?

'You didn't lead me on. Compared with many girls of
your age when they come on holiday, you're noticeably
reserved. If you were less attractive, I would have concluded that you hadn't much experience with men.'

Valissa hesitated. She was tempted to tell him that, in
the sense she thought he was referring to, she had none at
all. If he knew that, it would make it easier for him to
understand and forgive her behaviour the day before yesterday.

Instead, she said, 'Christopher Carter said that Greek
men probably regarded all foreign girls as amoral playgirls, game for anything. Is there some truth in that?'

'Some—yes,' he agreed. 'But if I had that idea about
you, I soon dismissed it. Playgirls make at least half the
running. In our case, I've done all the advancing and
most of the time you've been retreating. You have my

word I won't make another pass at you.'

'Why not?' she asked. 'I mean, if that was your intention before, why have you changed your mind?'

One hand on her shoulder, he turned her to face him. With the other he tilted her chin. 'Because there are many other things for men and women to enjoy together—friendship, laughter, swimming, eating and drinking. A relationship which depends on sex for its existence is not a rich one,' he answered, looking down at her with one of his more inscrutable expressions.

'No, agreed; but a relationship without sex is very unusual, not to say odd, at our age,' was Valissa's reaction.

'I don't say I will never kiss you,' Dion went on. 'But only like this.' He placed a chaste kiss on her forehead. 'How will that suit you?'

'F-fine,' she said uncertainly.

His white teeth gleamed in the sunlight as he threw back his head and laughed.

'Women are the most contrary creatures! You're disappointed—admit it.'

'No, I'm not. I'm just ... rather surprised,' she protested, her cheeks flushed.

'Let's go and have lunch.' Taking her hand, he led her back into the water.

She could see that he didn't believe her, and perhaps he was right. Perhaps she was disappointed.

The nicest of the waterfront restaurants was near where they had bathed, at the extreme end of the quay where the road turned at a right angle. Here, on a boarded floor, with a colourful awning overhead, about twenty or thirty tables had a grandstand view of the harbour and its comings and goings.

'You must be the only female passenger who hasn't done any shopping here,' said Dion, noticing some of their fellow passengers arriving at the restaurant laden with parcels.

'I've already done it all in Gaios,' she answered, remembering the ram's head ring and wondering if it was still for sale.

The waiter came and took their order. When they were alone again, Dion said, 'I did some shopping there this

morning. I hope you'll like what I bought for you.'
He took from his pocket a small box which he put on the
table in front of her.

'A present? How kind of you, Dion!' She braced herself
to show enthusiasm whatever the box might contain. It
was obviously a ring; perhaps one of the silver rams' heads
of which she had seen various types, some with curled
horns and some with swept back horns.

She opened the box and removed a piece of protective
wadding.

It was indeed a ram's head ring, but not one of the
cheap silver ones. It was the gold ring she had coveted.

'*Dion!*' she gasped, astounded. 'Oh, my goodness! Oh,
what possessed you to buy something so extravagant? It's
beautiful . . . gorgeous . . . but I can't possibly accept it.'

'It is the one you wanted, isn't it? The man in the shop
assured me it was the one you had tried on and liked.'

'Yes, I did like it—very much. But it's far too expensive
for a keepsake. I'm touched by your generosity, but——'

'It isn't a keepsake,' he interrupted. 'That's a parting
gift. This ring is not. It's for the future . . . our future. I
want you to marry me, Valissa.'

CHAPTER FIVE

THE ring had taken her breath away. But this—this was totally shattering.

While she sat, dumfounded with shock, Dion reached across the table to take both her hands in a strong clasp.

'I want you, Valissa—not just for a few nights of pleasure, for the rest of my life. To be the mother of my sons. I love you, and I think you love me. Let me put this ring on for you now. Then as soon as it can be arranged you shall have another—a wedding ring.'

Before she could recover her wits, he had taken the ring from its box and, after removing Nick's ring, replaced it with the golden ram's head. Then he put the Gemini ring on the third finger of her right hand and pressed his lips to her palms, one after the other.

'Spending yesterday without you was very salutary. I felt as if I had lost a part of myself. I——' He broke off as the waiter returned with bread and wine. After some instruction from Dion he took the bottle away with him.

'It's asking too much to expect them to have any champagne here, but I've ordered a bottle of something rather better than the house wine in which to drink to a long, happy life together,' Dion explained.

Valissa began to pull herself together. 'Aren't you being a little impetuous? You've known me such a short time. Shouldn't you wait a little longer before——'

He gave an impatient shake of the head. 'We are neither of us children. To wait and see is necessary for very young people because they don't know themselves as a more mature person does. If a man knows himself then he won't make a mistake in choosing a woman to suit him, and vice versa.'

She was silent; torn between an exultant happiness because he wanted to marry her, and the most profound doubt that a marriage was possible between them. Apart from anything else, how could she leave England as long as her grandfather was alive?

'Now you see why it is that I could promise to behave with the greatest restraint,' Dion said teasingly. 'Because very soon we shall be able to sleep together without offending the most strict moral code.' He leaned towards her, his eyes ardent. 'Are you as eager to spend a night in my arms as I am to have you there?'

She nodded, flushing a little. 'But, Dion, as you said earlier, a good relationship depends on much more than that. However much we ... we desire each other, there are other aspects to consider. Our backgrounds are so very different. Can they possibly mesh? *How* can they?'

'Tomorrow is time enough for thinking about practical matters. Today is reserved for being happy. Ah, here comes our wine,' he said cheerfully.

It was a much finer wine than any she had tasted before in Greece. More potent as well. One glass was enough to allay her misgivings, and make her surrender to the euphoria of lunching at the sea's edge with the most dynamic and gorgeous man she had ever laid eyes on; with the ring she had longed to take home with her now gleaming brightly on her finger, not as a piece of self-indulgence but as a token of his love.

It was not until early evening, after they had returned from Gaios to Loggos in Dion's boat—passing his cottage but not stopping there—that they were able to exchange the first proper kiss of the day.

No sooner had he closed the door of her apartment behind him than he swept her into his arms, and pressed a long, passionate kiss on her willing mouth.

'Intoxicating girl; you go to my head far more powerfully than any wine,' he told her huskily.

They drew apart, smiling at each other.

'Do you realise that I don't know your surname,' Valissa remarked.

An odd change came over his face. A look of unease,

swiftly masked. 'My mother's name was Stephanides.'

'Your mother's name?' she echoed, puzzled. Then she understood and, sensing his discomfiture, said quickly, 'Where shall we eat tonight? In one of the tavernas? Or do you want to test my culinary abilities?'

'If you can't cook now, you will learn. And I think it's better if we dine in public. My intentions are honourable, but being alone with you must always be a strain on them,' he said, with a return to his normal manner.

That he had obliquely admitted to illegitimacy meant nothing to Valissa. But she could appreciate that it might not be a matter of indifference to him. It surprised her a little that there should have been any children born out of wedlock on Paxos thirty-three years ago. She would have supposed that, in those days, any girl who became pregnant before marriage would have had a husband before the baby arrived. There must have been some special reason why Dion's father had not married his mother. Perhaps he had been lost at sea as fishermen must be occasionally.

She wondered if being fatherless had made Dion's childhood unhappy. Tourism had modernised Paxos to some extent, but plainly the inland villages were still years behind the modern world in amenities, and in the people's outlook. One-parent families might be a commonplace in more sophisticated societies, but she had a feeling that, when Dion was small, any boy without a father would still have been stigmatised as a bastard by the Paxiots.

The thought of him being made the scapegoat for his parents' foolishness filled her with anger, and a fierce desire to make it up to him for any hurts he had suffered as a child.

It was this which prompted her to seize one of his hands and press it to her cheek. 'I love you,' she murmured. 'I love you so much, Dion.'

'Even though I have very little to offer you?' His expression was sombre again.

'You have everything to offer, my darling. You're a *man*, which most of the men in my world aren't. Civilisation has emasculated them. They jog and diet to keep fit, but they couldn't survive if the oil ran dry, and modern life ground to a standstill, and we had to revert to the 'd ways. You could. You wouldn't starve.'

'In Paxos some of the old ways are still the only ways,' he said, with a laugh. 'I'm going to go down and order a lobster for our supper. You want to have a shower, I expect. Don't lock the front door in case I come back before you've finished.'

His quip about the island's backwardness reminded her of her earlier qualms. As she went for her shower she thought it would have been nice, for a change, to sink into a warm, scented bath and soak for a while. Here that was an impossibility because of the acute water shortage.

Among the typed list of advice and instructions which Andrew had compiled for the benefit of friends who borrowed or rented the apartment, there was one which read—*It saves water if, when showering, you first wet yourself, turn OFF water while lathering, turn ON water to rinse off. The water in the pipe will be tepid. However hot you are, please DON'T wait for it to run cold.*

Marriage to Dion would make baths a thing of the past. But which made for deep, dreamless sleep; a hot bath last thing at night, or a bed warmed by a loving husband?

All the comforts of her London flat had not prevented her from being very lonely in it at times. Work had been an effective anodyne in the past because, as she realised now, her deepest emotions had become paralysed by the shock and pain of losing Nick. But now that Dion had reanimated them, how could she bear to return to that withdrawn, work-dominated existence she had led for so long?

He rapped on the door. 'I'm back. The lobster is organised.'

'Great! I'll be out in a minute.'

Valissa ceased her absentminded shampooing and turned on the water to rinse off the suds, and the salt on her skin from bathing at Parga.

It would have been a memorable evening had they not been celebrating their engagement.

To Valissa's amazement, there was a bottle of Cristal Roederer 1974 to drink with the lobster.

'Never tell me a taverna in Loggos can produce a champagne of this order!' she expostulated when, having tasted it, she looked at the label. Although the blue plastic plant pot which had been brought into use as an ice bucket might have misled a more naïve girl, her grand-father had taught her enough about fine wines for her to recognise the outstanding quality of this one.

Dion's golden-grey eyes glinted with laughter. 'No, this was a stroke of luck. The skipper of the charter yacht which put in this afternoon'—with a nod in the direction of the sleek vessel lying at anchor—'happens to be a crony of mine. The people who pay for a cruise in her don't drink *Fix* or plonk with their meals. I asked him to sell me a couple of bottles of their tipple. They won't miss them. They have cases on board.'

'It's nectar,' she said appreciatively. 'You seem given to very expensive impulses, Dion. This beautiful, ex-travagant ring you've bought for me, and now champagne and lobster for supper.'

'It's a once-in-a-lifetime occasion. I have never before been betrothed,' he answered.

It was only very rarely that he expressed himself in a way which reminded her that English was a foreign lan-guage to him.

'I suppose I shall have to learn Greek,' she said. 'It's rather a daunting undertaking, what with the different alphabet, and a spoken and a written language.'

'Modern Greek isn't half as difficult as it looks, once you've spent about an hour on the alphabet and mastered the letters which are different. Not all of them are. The pronunciation is fairly straightforward, though the grammar is more complicated than English grammar. But you're an intelligent girl. You'll soon pick it up,' Dion said easily.

Valissa was not sure she shared his confidence. A girl she had been at school with, whose marriage had taken her to Spain, had told her that her grasp of Spanish had been hampered by having no one congenial to talk to.

'As we live in a country area,' Marigold had told her, last time they had lunched together in London, 'all our neighbours are peasant farmers—sweet people, but very simple in outlook. Mostly they speak a dialect which isn't at all like standard Spanish. Having quickly picked up basic Spanish—enough for shopping and so on—I find that I'm making no progress because of a dearth of women who can talk about anything but their children and what they saw on TV last night.'

Now, recalling that conversation, Valissa could visualise herself having the same problem. Gone for ever, if she lived here, would be the enthralling shop-talk which was life-blood to any career girl.

Gone, too, her career, come to that. People said 'what you never have, you never miss', and in Nick's time her career had been something to help make ends meet and fill in the years until he had established himself.

Subsequently, she had taken it more seriously. It had filled her life to the exclusion of most of the other things which young women did out of working hours. Wouldn't she be bound to miss it now?

Their lobster arrived, to a murmur of envious Oohs from people at other tables who were dining on less rarefied fare.

As the wine had at lunch-time, the champagne began to have its well-known effect of making no problems too weighty, no difficulties insuperable.

When Dion raised his glass in an unspoken toast, she gave him a radiant smile, her misgivings temporarily forgotten on this first unforgettable night of their whirlwind engagement.

Later when, from somewhere nearby, the throbbing notes of *bouzoukia* were added to the buzz of conversation, Dion sprang up and pulled her to her feet.

'I'll teach you to dance. You must learn to dance for our wedding.'

In the open space beyond the tables, he laid his arm along her shoulders and began the first slow, dragging steps.

'May we join in?' The question came from a young English couple.

'Sure. The more the merrier,' he said, grinning, looking towards the other diners.

Soon there were eight people in the line, some having

tried it before, some being tyros like Valissa. Dion shouted something in Greek to a Paxiot youth who was watching, and he ran forward to join on the end.

When the dance was over, and everyone but Dion and the local youth had collapsed in their chairs, panting for breath, an elderly man said to his wife, 'There'll be nothing like this going on at home tonight, Pamela—even if they are having an Indian Summer. I suppose that damned raucous disco will be making a racket as usual, but it's a long time since any of our young people have danced with the joie de vivre of these Greek chaps.'

Dion bowed to him. 'Thank you, sir. But why not join in yourself?'

'No, I'm far too old, my dear fellow. Can't spring about the way you can. Could at one time. Not any more.'

But he did, before the evening was over. Spurred by the lively example of a Greek much older than himself, the Englishman joined the line and acquitted himself with such vigour that his wife became worried in case he brought on a seizure.

Not surprisingly, the sound of merrymaking on the waterfront attracted the attention of the charter party on the yacht. Having finished a several-course meal on the candlelit deck, they rowed over to join in the fun.

They were an American couple, with two very glamorous daughters, who had set out from Athens to cruise through the Gulf of Corinth and then island-hop to Corfu.

When Dion had said that the skipper of the yacht was a crony of his, Valissa had assumed he was a Greek. However, both the skipper and his mate were blond and blue-eyed men. The third member of the crew was a girl, the sister of the mate. She was the cook.

'She's Cordon Bleu-trained, so we have the most fabulous meals,' said Nancy, the younger of the American girls, who imparted these details to Valissa.

'She's so nice. They all are—just darling. Rod, our skipper, is actually Sir Roderick Vale, an English baronet. His title goes way, way back, but he's the most unassuming person. You'd never guess he had an aristocratic background. My father and mother just love him. He has beautiful manners, and he's made this such a great trip.'

She went on to describe the wonder of the Corinth Canal. Valissa listened, and wondered if Nancy's parents were hoping that their skipper might become their son-in-law. He and the elder girl looked as if there could be something warmer than friendship between them. But it was not his friendship with Carol-Ann but Dion's with him which interested her.

When, after more dancing, she found herself standing near him, she introduced herself. 'Hello. I'm Valissa Cornford. You and Dion are old friends, I hear?'

For an instant it seemed to her that his blue eyes looked oddly blank, as if he didn't know what she was talking about. But it must have been her imagination, because almost at once he said warmly, 'I'm delighted to meet you, Valissa. How are you liking Paxos?'

'Very much, thank you. Even without meeting Dion, I should have enjoyed myself here,' she answered.

An arm slid round her waist. Dion said, 'I forgot to tell you, darling: most of my friends know me as Stefano—from my surname Stephanides. A name like Dionysius is regarded as a bit of a joke outside Greece, you know. I don't think, when I was crewing for you, that I ever admitted to it, did I, Rod?'

The other man grinned. 'No, you didn't. Dionysius, eh? Well, it's not as bad as Adonis. You had me foxed for a second, Valissa. I couldn't think who "Dion" was.'

'If most people know you as Stefano, why did you tell me to call you Dion?' she asked, slightly puzzled.

'It's what I was called as a small boy, by my mother and my grandparents . . . all the people who were closest to me. As you're going to be even closer, it seemed the appropriate one for you to use,' he explained, smiling down at her. 'Valissa and I are going to be married, Rod.'

'You are?' His friend's sun-bleached eyebrows shot up in surprise. 'That's splendid! Congratulations, Stefano. If Valissa is as charming as she looks, you're a very lucky fellow. And you're lucky, too, Valissa. I've been in several kinds of trouble with this guy, and I can't think of anyone better to have around in a tight spot whether it's a Force

Ten gale or ... well, I won't go into details of all the contingencies we've survived together'—with another grin at Dion. 'But you can take my word for it, he's a sound chap in an emergency.'

'I know it. That's how we met. He rescued me from the sea.' she said.

'Really? What happened?' asked Roderick.

'Nothing worthy of the term rescue,' Dion answered for her. 'Valissa's outboard had failed and I gave her a tow in, that's all.'

Roderick said, 'How long have you two known each other? Are you working on the island?'—to her.

She shook her head.

Dion said, 'We met just over a week ago, and we've been engaged about ten hours.'

As Roderick's eyebrows shot even higher than before, a voice said, 'Did I hear an engagement mentioned?' and they were joined by Nancy's mother.

Roderick introduced them to her. Her name was Lillian.

She said, 'This calls for a celebration. Let's all go back on board and open some champagne. Irving, honey, come over and meet these two young people who've just gotten engaged to be married.'

Valissa had an intuition that Lillian wanted to throw an impromptu party for them because she felt it might put Roderick in the mood to emulate his Greek friend. However, if the American woman had an ulterior motive for being hospitable, it was still fun to visit the luxurious yacht where Janie, the cook, quickly produced some savoury titbits to eat with the champagne.

'I have the feeling we've met before, Stefano,' their host said to Dion, when they were all sitting on deck. 'Is that possible?'

Dion shook his head. 'I don't think so.' His tone was casual.

But Valissa noticed that Roderick shot a swift look at him, a guarded look which she interpreted as meaning that *he* thought they could have met before, perhaps in circumstances which were better forgotten. If that were the case, surely Dion would have found some reason to avoid coming aboard?

Yet there was, she felt, something forced in Roderick's jocular remark, 'You'll see a dozen like him on any Greek waterfront. It's the curly hair and the weatherbeaten look which are familiar.'

'I wouldn't call him weatherbeaten. I wish I could tan that colour,' said Carol-Ann.

The light of the storm-shaded candles emphasised that Dion's skin was many tones darker than anyone else's.

'And Stefano is taller than most Greeks, and he doesn't have dark eyes. Irving has a phenomenal memory for faces. If he thinks you've met before, I'd say he's probably right—even if it was only that you passed each other in the street,' added Lillian.

'It's possible. I've been to San Francisco and various other American ports.' Dion still sounded unconcerned.

'It'll come to me. Give me time,' said his host. 'If I put my mind to work on a problem of any kind last thing at night, in the morning I awake knowing the answer. Did you realise you could make your subconscious work for you in that way, Valissa?'

'No, I didn't.'

'You should try it. It's most effective. In fact I attribute a great deal of my success in life to the power of my subconscious.'

Ignoring his younger daughter's irreverent giggle, Irving began to elaborate on his theory.

It was after midnight when Dion took Valissa ashore and escorted her to the door of the apartment.

In spite of his promise at Parga that he would not attempt to make love to her until they were married, she wondered if kissing her goodnight would weaken his resolution. Perhaps he knew it would. Instead of taking her in his arms, he confined himself to kissing her hands—the backs, the knuckles, the palms, the soft skin inside her wrists.

Even that made her quiver with longing to experience again the caresses against which she had struggled two days ago.

'Until tomorrow, my love,' was his final husky good-night, before he strode swiftly away.

As she had on the night they had met, she watched for him from her roof terrace. The waterfront was silent and deserted now, although on the charter yacht lights still shone from the cabins with ports to starboard.

As before, Dion rowed away from the quay and, to her surprise, instead of making for the open sea, he seemed to be going back to the yacht. Then there was a movement on deck and she saw Roderick's figure emerge from a patch of shadow. As the dinghy slid alongside, he swung himself on to the boarding ladder and Dion stood up and grasped the handrail. For several minutes they talked, being close enough to keep their voices very low and not be overheard by anyone else on board.

There was something decidedly conspiratorial about the two men having a conversation very late at night when everyone else on the yacht was preparing for bed. Valissa wished she knew what they were saying.

Eventually Dion resumed his seat on the thwart, and Roderick climbed back on deck and, with a final lift of the hand, disappeared below.

Soon after sunrise next morning, Valissa went to the nearby beach and found the yacht's skipper there before her. He was not alone. Irving and Janie's brother were in the water. Roderick had been swimming but now was drying himself.

When the sound of her feet on the pebbles attracted his attention, he came across to say a friendly good morning to her.

'You're another early riser, are you? Lillian and the girls like to greet the day rather later, although Janie will be up by now. She'll be busy preparing the breakfast.'

'I've had my first swim at this hour every day since I've been here,' Valissa told him. 'Has Irving's subconscious revealed to him when and where he saw Dion before?'

'If it has, he hasn't mentioned it yet. I doubt if he's seen him, actually.'

'How long have you and Dion . . . Stefano known each other?'

'Years. Since we were kids. My parents were some of the first foreigners to discover Paxos.'

'You must think it's rather reckless of him to propose to a girl he's known such a short time, don't you?'

He parried the question. 'Do you feel it's reckless of you to have accepted him?'

'Yes, I suppose I do. If another girl were in my place, I should probably think her crazy,' she admitted. 'But I should envy her as well.'

'I don't think you need have any qualms. If I had a sister, I should be happy to see her married to Stefano. He . . . he may not seem much of a catch in the worldly sense, but if you want a man with guts and a great sense of humour, you've got one in him. Have you fixed a date for the wedding?'

'No, we haven't discussed any of the practical details yet.'

'If I know Stefano, there won't be too many details,' said Roderick. 'If your mother is an equally strong character, determined to see you married with all the traditional panoply, I fancy you're going to find yourself in the middle of a head-on collision. Although they do say love works wonders and, if *you* want a fashionable wedding, he may go along with it.'

'My only family is my grandfather. If I did have that type of mother, I imagine she would resist any kind of wedding to a Paxiot. As you said yourself, Dion isn't exactly what most people mean by eligible. Oh, look, there he is!'—pointing at the boat which had come into view round the point.

Roderick cupped his hands round his mouth and hallooed to attract his friend's attention.

Dion waved, but he didn't change course. Valissa guessed he would leave his boat in the harbour and walk over the hill to join them.

She was in the water when he arrived, and Irving and Bill were drying themselves, with Roderick sitting by waiting for them. Dion had a few words with the three men, then stripped off his jeans and waded in the sea to join her.

Treading water, they exchanged a light kiss. Later, when they came out, there was no one else to see him draw her wet body to him and kiss her more hungrily.

Presently, as they walked back over the hill, his arm round her waist, he said, 'How much notice must you give before you can leave your job and we can be married?'

'A month, but I think this is something we need to discuss.'

'What is there to discuss? You can't go on working when we are married. You'll have your hands full being my wife. I shall want your undivided attention,' he said, smiling down at her.

'But, Dion, that may not be possible, at least not immediately. What shall we live on? Can you earn enough to support two people?'

'Naturally. I shouldn't have asked you to be my wife if I couldn't look after you. As far as the wedding is concerned, I think it should take place in England so that your grandfather can be present. From what you've told me, he's not strong enough to travel far.'

'What about all your relations? Don't you want any of them to be there?'

'From my point of view the quietest and quickest form of marriage is the best. It's our honeymoon which interests me. Where shall we go for our first nights of love?'

'I don't know. It will be November by then—not a very nice month in England. Even here it will be much colder, won't it? How cold and how rainy, Dion?'

'In November? We have a fair amount of rain—maybe ten days or a little more—but it isn't particularly cold. On the dry days it will be sunny, and at night I will keep you warm'—his arm tightening, his eyes desirous.

Valissa could not but be pleased at his eagerness to possess her. At the same time she felt they were skirting important issues which would have to be thrashed out sooner or later. Maybe Greek women—at least in the more remote places such as Paxos—weren't expected to know what their husbands earned.

But Valissa—although a middle-of-the-road person in

matters of sex equality—had been her own mistress for
too long to be able to accept total dependence on her
husband.

Encouraged by her grandfather, whose present comfortable way of life was the result of far-sighted investment
at a time when many of his contemporaries depended on
old-fashioned thrift to cushion their retirement years, she
had for long taken an intelligent interest in money matters. She was not about to surrender this habit of mind
and leave all that side of life to Dion.

However, she knew better than to broach a tricky subject before breakfast.

Before they had finished breakfast, Roderick came up
to the apartment to say goodbye.

'The forecast says there's a blow in the offing. Nothing
much, but possibly enough to make Lillian and Nancy
queasy if we delay the crossing to Corfu. So we're off to
take a quick look at Lakka and then skedaddle north,' he
explained. 'Irving's subconscious has definitely failed him
this time,' he added. 'He still can't place you, Stefano.'

Dion shrugged. 'I never thought he would. My memory
for faces isn't bad, and I've never laid eyes on him before,
although I've seen his trucks in the States.' He stood up
and gripped his friend's hand. 'It's been great running
into you, Roderick. Give my regards to your mother when
you get home.'

'Not long now. Only another month or so and then it's
back to "England, home and beauty", thank God.'

'You would rather be there than here?' Valissa asked,
surprised.

'No question!' was his emphatic answer. 'These islands
in winter are bloody awful, if you ask me.'

He realised he had said something tactless, and was
quick to add, 'But I'm a prejudiced witness because, if it
weren't for the money I make out of chartering to dollar
millionaires, I'd never set foot out of Northamptonshire.
In fact, apart from going outside to meets, I could happily
live and die without leaving my own "blessed plot", to
use Shakespeare's phrase.'

'But as Roderick's plot extends to several thousand
acres, and his home is a country house worthy of being

protected for posterity by the National Trust, his is rather an exceptional case,' was Dion's dry comment.

'Really? What is your house called?' asked Valissa, having visited most of the National Trust's properties within easy reach of London.

He told her, adding, 'You know that if either or both of you are ever anywhere near us, Mother and I will always be delighted to see you. I won't suggest that you invite us to the wedding because knowing you, dear old chap, it'll be a special licence, minimum fuss and bother affair.'

They were all on the terrace. Glancing at the yacht lying in the harbour below, he said, 'Must dash now—not my own master here, you know. Goodbye, Valissa. Mama will be agog to hear that the partner-in-crime of my schooldays is about to surrender his freedom. She thinks I should, too.'

He kissed her on both cheeks, slapped Dion's shoulder and departed.

'I suppose being friendly with Roderick when you were children was the foundation of your incredibly good English?' said Valissa, when he had gone.

It would also account for the fact that, mingled with his almost inperceptible Greek accent, were the drawn-out vowels of the English landed gentry.

Dion's response was a somewhat absentminded nod.

'I'll make some more coffee, shall I?' Without waiting for his assent, she went to the kitchen.

Was it true, as Roderick had said, that the islands—so idyllic in summer—were indeed "bloody awful" in the winter?

She had the impression that in recent years Corfu had become an all year round resort. But spending a fortnight's holiday in a centrally-heated hotel with up-to-date plumbing was a different matter from living all winter in an unheated, uninsulated cottage at the back of beyond.

When she returned to the terrace, Dion had moved their chairs so that they could watch the yacht leaving harbour.

'Does Roderick make a small fortune chartering?' she asked.

'I believe so. He wouldn't do it if it were not worthwhile

financially. Ocean-cruising was his father's passion, and he spent more money on it than he should have done. When he died, three years ago, Lady Vale was left in relatively straitened circumstances. Fortunately, because of its outstanding features, the Trust took on the house without the usual endowment. Roderick wanted to sell the yacht, which had been his father's final extravagance, but he was advised to hang on to it for the time being.'

'I suppose he can charge higher rates because of the snob-appeal of his title?'

'You know about that, do you?'

'Nancy told me. I suspect her mother has matrimonial ambitions for Carol-Ann.'

'She's wasting her time. He's been a target for match-making mothers for far too long to be caught now. Besides, he's in love with a girl who he knows for certain doesn't give a damn about his title—would prefer him without it, in fact.'

'Why is that?'

'Because she's in the unusual position of having inheri-ted a barony dating back to 1300-and-something. At the moment they're at an impasse because she's as crazy about her family's house as Roderick is about his place. Neither of them is prepared to give way, but to keep up both places—particularly when they have the extra drain of school fees—is not on. If there is a compromise, they haven't found it yet.'

Valissa said, 'Speaking of compromises, I was wondering if—as you're a jack-of-all-trades with no very rigid work ties—we might reach one ourselves. I mean, if what Roderick said is true, and the islands are rather hellish in winter, I wonder if it might be better to spend our sum-mers in Greece and our winters in my flat in London?'

'Roderick exaggerates. The climate here is a damned sight preferable to the winter months in North-amptonshire. He doesn't notice the weather there unless it's bad enough to stop him hunting, and then he holes up in his library, catching up with the issues of *Country Life* which he missed during the summer. He's obses-sional about England; it's partly a reaction to his father's obsession with the Mediterranean.'

'I don't think I'm obsessional about England. I love Abroad,' she said mildly. 'But it does seem foolish to give up a nice little flat, and a job which I'm doing rather well at, and could probably continue part-time in the sense of part of each year.'

'And what do you suggest I should do with myself during those times?'

'I don't know. But there must be any number of possibilities.'

'No, it wouldn't work,' he said decisively. 'In the first place I think you'd have difficulty in continuing your job on a winter-on, summer-off basis; and to spend half the year cooped up in a flat in London wouldn't suit me at all.'

'But, Dion, I might as well say that to spend my winters in your cottage wouldn't suit *me*. We can't consider our future only in terms of our own preferences. We have to make allowances for each other's needs.'

'And our children's needs. I should like to have a family. Perhaps you don't want to have babies—I know some women don't nowadays.'

'I do. I shall be very happy to be the mother of your sons,' she said gently, hoping the reminder of his own words to her at Parga would restore him to his usual good humour.

She was not used to seeing him look sternly at her.

'Then as you're almost twenty-four, and I'm in my thirties, we have no time to waste,' was his answer.

'But can we afford to start a family right away? I'm not clear what your future plans are . . . or what money you have in reserve . . . or anything,' she ended, with a gesture of uncertainty.

Leaning towards her, Dion captured her outspread hands and enclosed them firmly in his.

'Last night when I spoke of having little to offer you in material terms, you told me it didn't matter—that what you wanted was a man who could survive in the most basic sense, and ensure your survival. Are you having second thoughts now, Valissa? Has seeing how people like Irving and his wife live made you think you would prefer a more de luxe life-style?'

'No, no—that's not true,' she protested. 'I've seen plenty of luxury living. Only rich people can afford to have Eliot Rutherford-designed houses, but the wives aren't always happy women. Sometimes, if you catch them at an unguarded moment, they look acutely unhappy. You don't have to tell me that love and good health and enough to eat are the fundamentals of happiness.'

'Then why are you worried about our future together? Why not trust me? Do you think that, loving you, I would fail to provide for you—and not merely the essentials, but anything else you needed to complete your contentment?'

The renewal of tenderness in his manner which, moments before, had been alarmingly steely, brought a shimmer of tears to her eyes.

'Oh, darling, I do trust you—truly,' she told him, a break in her voice.

He sprang up, pulling her with him, folding her tightly in his arms.

'Don't cry, foolish girl. There's nothing to cry for.'

'I'm not . . . not really,' she mumbled. 'It's just that . . . being happy like this is so new to me that I—I can't bear anything to spoil it.'

He tilted her face up to his. 'Nothing need spoil it—if you'll trust me.'

Through damp lashes Valissa saw his dark face, every lean forceful line indicative of strength of character. At that moment it seemed crazy to doubt for a second that, as his wife, she would ever be anything but totally secure, totally cherished.

'I do . . . I will,' she breathed unsteadily.

Then his mouth closed possessively on hers, sweeping aside all doubt, all uncertainty, with the overwhelming force of his physical power over her.

The next day, a little diffidently, Valissa asked if they could go to the cottage for her to measure the rooms and make sketches with a view to redesigning the interior.

She felt Dion was not entirely in favour of this proposal, but after some moments' consideration, he shrugged and agreed.

Her second impression of the cottage was not encouraging. Before, she had been too shaken up by her recent ordeal to take in many details. But now, in full daylight, and assessing the possibilities with professional detachment, her conclusion was that Eliot would consider it a hovel, and its only virtue its position overlooking the sea.

As if he guessed something of what was in her mind, Dion said, 'Perhaps, in a year or two, we shall be able to build a new house here. In the south of France and parts of Spain a site with this view would command an extremely high price. Even here, land prices are rising.'

'Yes, it's a wonderful site—provided the road from here to the main road is not too rough and winding,' she qualified. 'The big snag about building new houses or renovating old ones on islands is that usually many of the materials have to be brought from somewhere else. That adds considerably to the cost. For instance, these inward-opening windows are never reliably watertight, and——'

'That's why there are shutters,' he cut in.

'Yes, but who wants to have to close shutters every time the sky looks threatening? Also they're difficult to curtain. Unless he is dealing with clients who are on what he calls "a peasant kick", Eliot always persuades them to replace all original windows with modern aluminium sliding ones. They may be less "in keeping", but they're twenty times more practical.'

Dion's firm mouth tightened. 'I hope Eliot is not going to be too pervasive an influence in our lives,' he said, with an edge of sarcasm.

She flushed. 'That's unfair! I'm not constantly talking about Eliot, but his name is bound to crop up in any discussion about houses.'

She knew it had been ill-advised to let slip Eliot's term for people who embraced the simple life to the point of absurdity. For a moment she had forgotten that Dion was the grandson of peasants; that his grandmother had probably covered her hair with the draped headcloth still worn by older women in the smaller villages. His grandfather might even have worn the *vraca*, the baggy breeches of fishermen in days gone by.

'Frankly I think it would be better to leave all this measuring until later. You have only a few more days here. Let's enjoy ourselves,' Dion said impatiently.

'But later will be too late. If I don't buy curtain materials and lampshades and rugs in London, where shall I buy them? Not in Gaios, I feel sure.'

'Probably not, but it's possible we may not come back here for the winter. I don't mean I'm changing my mind about living in London,' he added briskly. 'There are places where the weather in winter is as good as it is here in summer. Maybe we'll try our luck in one of those.'

'Try our luck?' she echoed doubtfully.

'Perhaps in one of the Caribbean islands. You'd have no complaints about their climate.'

'But where would we live . . . and what on?'

'We'd manage. There's money to be made out of sail-boarding.'

'Teaching people to use them, you mean?'

'And selling them.'

Valissa's heart sank. If she had been eighteen or nineteen, and he only a year or two older, the prospect of adventuring round the world with him would have filled her with excited anticipation. But not now; not if he wanted her to start a baby as soon as possible.

Maybe children brought up like little gypsies by carefree, improvident parents who never planned more than a week ahead were as happy—possibly happier—as children with more settled lives.

But as Dion had said to her at Parga, people of her age and his age were fully mature and self-knowing. She knew her own nature too well to delude herself that she could enjoy being pregnant while having no idea where the child was to be born, or where they would live after its birth.

'I think that would only be postponing the moment when we have to buckle down to reality, Dion. Surely if Paxos is where your roots are, where you want your children to grow up, the sooner we tackle the job of making this place into a comfortable home, the better it will be. Teach sailboarding here, next summer, and meanwhile apply all that muscle'—touching his arm, and smiling at him—'to renovating the cottage.'

'All right: if that's what you want. But finish the measuring later. At this moment I want to kiss you, and then to swim.' He pulled her to him.

That night, after he had left her, she looked at the incomplete floor plan which she ought to have finished that morning, together with photographs and sketches as detailed reminders of exactly how the cottage looked for when she was back in London.

Dion could not fly there with her. He had things to do in Athens, and would join her about two weeks later.

'Some business with one of my cousins,' had been his evasive reply, when she had asked why he was visiting the capital.

She had not liked to press him for details. He had shown no interest in her affairs—her salary, the cost of her flat, the extent of her mortgage, etcetera—which made it awkward to question him closely. But she couldn't help feeling that their management of their finances was a matter which a couple soon to be married should discuss very fully and frankly.

On the surface, her last days in Paxos were a period of idyllic happiness. From their breakfasts together on her terrace to the *ouzos* they drank in the evening, the sunlit hours passed like a golden daydream.

Dion made her laugh. He made her feel beautiful. Often he made her tremble with longing for the consummation of their love. Yet ardent as he was, he never overstepped the limit he had imposed on himself. His restraint amazed and reassured her, for she saw it as evidence of his seriousness. He must love her very deeply to be able to control the passion she knew she aroused in him.

She needed that reassurance because, deep down, she was still uneasy. Perhaps she knew, all along, that it was too perfect to last.

Afterwards, the sudden, explosive quarrel which, on her last day, shattered their harmony, reminded her of the squall which had caused them to meet in the first place.

They were in the apartment at the time, and for several minutes the sound of their raised, angry voices could probably be heard in the street below.

Their hostilities didn't last long. They ended when Valissa was driven to removing the ring he had given her, and holding it out to him.

'I think you'd better have this back. I think we've both made a mistake.'

CHAPTER SIX

DION stared at her, silent and grim-faced.

At last, his voice quiet and controlled, he said, 'I think we need time to cool down. I'm going out for a while, but I'll be back.'

When he had gone, she looked at the ring she was holding between the middle finger and thumb of her right hand. Then she put it on a table and walked outside on to the terrace, knowing the past few days had been a fool's paradise.

That they could have so fierce a dispute within a short time of declaring their love for each other made her realise how frail it had been, the apparent rapport between them.

Clearly, Dion wanted a wife who would yield to his judgment in everything; equally clearly she could not. She had been an independent adult for too long to accept having her opinions dismissed, her wishes overruled simply because he was a male and she was a female. It was ante-diluvian, his attitude. Totally unacceptable.

He was gone for an hour. When he came back, Valissa was packing. Although her flight did not leave Corfu airport until late the following afternoon, the ferry left Gaios at half past seven in the morning and was expected to call at Loggos before eight.

When he walked through the door, she had just laid a skirt in the case. She straightened and faced him, wondering what sort of mood he was in now.

He came straight to where she was standing, and put both hands on her shoulders.

'Are you ready to kiss and make up? I am.'

She shook her head. 'I'm sorry I lost my temper, but I can't take back the things I said. You *were* asking too much of me, Dion. All the concessions would have been on my side. You would have given up nothing.' She hoped he had noticed her deliberate use of the past tense. 'Unless you count your freedom as a sacrifice.'

'Oh, God!—You obstinate female,' he exclaimed, half amused, half exasperated. 'If you're prepared to take for granted that I won't beat you ... that I'll be a good father to your children ... why can't you trust me to provide for you? You will never want for anything you need, I give you my word. I swear it. But it's not something I can prove to you here and now. You've got to have faith in me ... trust me.'

Almost, he made her waver. Almost.

After a brief hesitation she gave a slight, despairing shake of the head.

'It's all happened much too fast, Dion. To commit ourselves for a lifetime on the strength of these few days together ... it's not on, I realise that now. If we could wait ... test our feelings ... but how can we do that, when you're a Greek and I'm English, and our lives just don't mesh in any way?'

'I don't need to test *my* feelings,' was his unhesitating answer. 'But if you're not certain ...'. He shrugged, and his strong hands dropped from her shoulders. 'At least let's be civilised about it, and part on good terms. Not in anger. You'll have dinner with me, won't you?'

Valissa had never felt less like eating, but she nodded. 'Yes ... very well.'

All through their last meal together, her throat ached with unshed tears. Such conversation as they had was like that of strangers rather than lovers.

Dion told her about the Greek submarine, *Papanikolis*, which, during the Second World War, had hidden in the Ipapandi cave on the west coast, emerging at night to torpedo enemy ships.

She asked him about the earthquakes which, before she was born and when he was still a small boy, had damaged or destroyed almost three-quarters of the buildings on the more southerly islands of Zakinthos, Cefalonia and Ithaca.

'Yes, it was a terrible disaster, but this island, and Corfu and Kithira, are not at risk. And even in Zante on Zakinthos, where the earthquake was followed by a fire when the wind fanned the embers of an overturned grill in one of the tavernas, the new town has been built to withstand another equally bad tremor.'

'All the same, it can't help the tourist trade,' said Valissa, laying down her fork with her stuffed pepper only half eaten. 'I'm sorry, I'm not very hungry tonight.'

'I know. Nor am I.'

He would have poured some more wine for her, but she shook her head. 'No, I don't want any more to drink. I— I think, if you wouldn't mind, I'll go back and get on with my packing. I should have dealt with it earlier.' Her voice shook as she strove to control the desolation inside her.

As she pushed back her chair, Dion rose and tossed some money on the table. They left the taverna together. He gave her no choice, putting his arm firmly round her as they turned their backs to the curious glances of the other diners, some of whom had joined in the dancing which he had started on the night of their engagement.

'I can't bear to see you upset. Must it end like this, darling?' he murmured, as he helped her to climb the steep steps from one lane to the other.

'Not if you would come with me to London. Why can't you, Dion? *Why can't you?*' she pleaded, as they reached the top. 'You told me yourself, the other day, that the population of these islands had been halved in the last sixty years because so many people had emigrated. If all those expatriate Greeks can make good new lives for themselves in America and Australia, why can't you come to England with me? What is it which binds you to Paxos?'

He took her face between his hands. 'It isn't what binds me to Paxos. I could leave here, and never come back—if I had to. If, for example, there was another outbreak of totalitarian government. It isn't that I must stay here, Valissa. It's that always, throughout history, men have led and women have followed. I can't alter my instincts in that respect.'

'To most civilised people marriage is a partnership between equals nowadays,' she said bitterly.

'To a great extent, yes. But women can't change their

physiology. They will always have to bear children. To expect them to be wives, mothers and breadwinners, all at the same time, is too much of a burden. Already they're suffering from stresses which I shan't allow with my wife.'

She knew it was futile to argue. His ideas were too deeply imbued.

'In life, as in love,' Dion said softly, 'occasionally it does no harm for the woman to take the initiative, to play the dominant part. But Nature made me taller and stronger for me to defend and protect you . . . for me to take and you to give. . . .'

His head bent and his mouth touched her cheek.

'Then take me,' she whispered. 'Take me. . . .'

As his arms crushed her to him, she knew she could not, twice in a lifetime, endure the torment of regret she had felt because she and Nick had never made love. She had to have one night with Dion; one night to remember for ever.

Deliberately, she parted her lips and made herself softer, more yielding.

If the door of the apartment had been unlocked, if she hadn't left one of the lamps alight, if he hadn't caught sight of his ring glinting on the table where she had put it; then she might have fulfilled her intention to cast aside every restraint.

But unlocking the door was a slight but significant interruption, and because the apartment was not in darkness it was different from entering a room with only a shaft of moonlight to guide them towards the divan.

Even then it might have worked, but for the ring. As Dion lowered her on to the couch and reluctantly broke off his kisses to reach out and turn off the light, they both saw the bright gleam of gold which had symbolised their shared future.

He picked it up, and made to replace it on her finger.

Quickly she withdrew her hand. 'No . . . I didn't mean that I . . . that we. . . .' she faltered.

A frown drew his dark eyebrows downwards. 'What did you mean?'

She put a hand up to his cheek. 'That I'd like you to stay here tonight.' Her hand slid to the back of his neck.

She swayed towards him. 'Don't stop kissing me, darling
. . . oh, Dion!' She breathed his name like a sigh, her eyes
soft with love and longing.

'Are you saying that you want me to stay here, but you
don't want to marry me, Valissa?'.

She nodded. 'But don't talk . . . kiss me.' Her fingers
delved in the curls at the back of his head, and she tried
to make him bend closer.

Dion resisted the pressure. He stopped her other hand
from slipping inside his shirt to smooth the bronzed skin
of his chest.

'No, that's not what I want,' he said firmly. 'When I
did want you on those terms, you told me that for you to
enjoy making love you had to be deeply committed.
That's the way I feel now about you. I no longer want
only your body. I want all of you . . . heart and soul.'

'You have my heart, Dion,' she murmured. 'I do love
you . . . but I can't marry you.'

'That's usually what men say to women when they want
to have their cake and eat it,' was his sardonic answer.
'I've always thought your sex were foolish to fall for that
pitch. I never thought I'd be on the receiving end of it.
Either way, there's still only one sensible answer.'

He had slipped the finely wrought ram's head over the
tip of his middle finger. Now he held it towards her.

'If you want to bed me, you'll have to wed me.'

Valissa was not the only passenger waiting to be picked
up by the caique the next morning. Four other people,
with an amazing amount of luggage, were also waiting on
the quay.

Until the very last moment, she half hoped that Dion
might appear, by sea or even by taxi; that he would
come with her; that they had not really seen the last of
each other.

Even when the boat called at Lakka to pick up some
more departing holidaymakers, she still felt a faint flicker
of hope that he might be among the waiting figures.

It was only when the caique put to sea again that she
knew they had parted for ever. What he had said to her
last night had been his final ultimatum. She had refused

it. There was no more to be said—only goodbye.

When the ferry arrived at Corfu, there was time to explore the capital before leaving for the airport. Valissa wandered aimlessly about the crowded streets for half an hour, then forced herself to have something to eat in a restaurant.

It was as well that she did, because her next meal was not, as she had anticipated, an early supper on the flight to London.

Her plane had begun its take-off when there was a slight lurching movement, caused by the brakes being applied. Shortly afterwards the captain announced that one of the engines was giving an unsatisfactory reading and a check was necessary. Would the passengers collect their hand luggage and return to the terminal building.

Several hours later, by which time they had been told they were going to have to wait for another aircraft to be flown out from Gatwick to collect them, Valissa and her companions were still hanging about in the small, scruffy, overcrowded airport, enviously watching other flights take off on time.

Until sunset it was very hot. At times there were not enough seats for everyone to sit down, and the drinks from the bar were no longer refreshingly cold because the demand for them was so heavy that there wasn't time for the cans to be properly chilled.

As Valissa was not being met at the other end, and had plenty of reading material with her, in the ordinary way she would have accepted the delay philosophically, feeling more sorry for the people with tired, fretful children than for herself.

However, in her present state of wretchedness, the noise and the lack of privacy were very hard to take.

Presently it was announced that dinner at a hotel had been laid on for them. They could stay there till midnight.

In the end it was half past one in the morning before, at last, they were airborne. The usual tray meal was served, after which some people dozed.

Valissa closed her eyes, but she couldn't sleep. It was now more than twenty-four hours since Dion had held her in his arms. It seemed like forever. How was she going to survive the weeks and months before the pain dulled?

At four o'clock in the morning, English time, she unlocked the door of her flat. She had left the bed made up with clean sheets. She set the alarm clock for seven-thirty. By then she was exhausted. Within seconds of climbing into bed, she was out like a light.

She had lunch with Elizabeth Barclay who, when she heard about the flight, said, 'You needn't have come to work today. Twenty-four hours in transit, and three hour's sleep! No wonder you don't look exactly rejuvenated by your holiday.'

'I'll make up the lost sleep tonight. Aren't you impressed by my tan? I'm not wearing tights today. They felt so peculiar after three weeks without them that, having put them on, I took them off again.' Valissa displayed a slim bare leg.

'Yes, you're marvellously brown.' Elizabeth asked about Paxos, but she didn't refer to the extra week's holiday.

It was Valissa herself who, feeling she owed the older woman an explanation, broached the subject by asking, 'What did Eliot have to say about my extension of leave?'

'He's extended his trip to the States, so he doesn't know about it yet. Anyway, the way you've devoted yourself to the job since you joined us, he can't quibble about a little extra time off.'

'I—I was almost persuaded to stay in Paxos permanently.'

In the act of lifting a forkful of salad to her lips, Elizabeth paused. 'Were you, indeed? I assumed he was also on holiday, but he lives there, I gather? What is he? A writer? An artist?'

'He called himself a jack-of-all-trades. He was a local . . . a Paxiot. His name was Dionysios Stefanides.'

Although it had never been her nature to confide in anyone but her grandparents, suddenly Valissa found herself telling Elizabeth the full story of her relationship with Dion, even to the circumstances leading to his final ultimatum.

'I find that most extraordinary,' said Elizabeth thoughtfully. 'Women have been holding out for a wedding ring since Anne Boleyn hooked Henry the Eighth by that method. It's not one which works too well nowadays, when girls who don't are outnumbered by those who do. But whoever heard of a man saying No?'

Valissa was already regretting this particular revelation. Not because she thought it would lower Elizabeth's opinion of her. Since a brief, unhappy marriage in her early twenties had ended in divorce, Elizabeth had had more than one lover. She was currently involved with a surgeon who couldn't persuade her to marry him because she could see herself having to surrender her career. He was a widower with three children. His mother ran his home, but was eager to bow out as soon as he could persuade Elizabeth or some other woman to replace her.

So Elizabeth, who regarded making love as a pleasure on a par with going to the opera or spending a day in the country, but not as a reason for sacrificing one's independence or taking on unwanted responsibilities, was not the kind of person to be shocked by Valissa inviting a man into her bed. Nevertheless it was an intensely personal thing to have admitted to her, and Valissa would not have done it if she hadn't been tired and overstrung.

'This row you had . . . when you gave him back his ring. What was that all about?' asked Elizabeth.

Valissa gave a hollow laugh. 'About plumbing, of all things.'

'Plumbing?'

'The plumbing in Paxos comes as a bit of a shock if one isn't forewarned. Perhaps if Andrew and Sue *had* warned me, I should have been put off going; which would have been a pity, because the island is lovely, and the one or two gruesome aspects aren't insupportable in a holiday context. At least not to me, there alone.'

'You don't mean the loos are old-fashioned earth-closets, do you? My goodness, in a hot climate——'

'No, it's not as bad as that, thank goodness, or not in any house I heard about.'

Valissa explained, causing Elizabeth to grimace with distaste. 'I couldn't put up with that for long. Why do they, for heaven's sake? Given an efficient septic tank and suitable pipes, a house at the back of beyond can have up-to-date plumbing.'

'That's what I told Dion about the cottage—that I couldn't live there without hot and cold water in the kitchen, and no sinister bucket in the bathroom.'

'I should think not,' Elizabeth agreed. 'You mean he expected you to accept all the inconveniences his grandmother had had to put up with?'

'Perhaps not. I'm not really sure. He was vague, and I was aggressive instead of persuasive. We rubbed each other the wrong way. It was as stupid as most quarrels.'

'It sounds to me as if Dion's ideas about women are as out of date as the island's plumbing. I can understand you falling for him, and obviously he was head over heels about you. It's not usually marriage which those bronzed Apollos have in mind. Was he the only interesting male around? Weren't there any attractive Englishmen?'

Valissa shook her head.

Three days later, Elizabeth came into her office and said, 'There's someone asking for you in the showroom. You've been holding out on me, Valissa. He's English, extremely personable, and you met him in Paxos. Doesn't the name Christopher Carter ring any bells?'

For a second or two it didn't, then she remembered him. The solicitor who had warned her against trusting Dion.

'Extremely personable?' she said doubtfully, remembering the reddened skin, the pompous manner, the too loose shorts and the thighs which were not brown and muscular.

But a few minutes later she discovered that Christopher in Sloane Street looked very different from Christopher in Gaios. Now, wearing a well-cut suit and strolling round the elegant showroom, he looked as much in his element as Dion had in the sunlit *platia*. How would Dion look here? Valissa wondered. Out of place, probably. But still a thousand times more welcome than this man.

'Hello, Christopher.' She forced a friendly smile.

He swung round, his eager expression becoming a stare of surprise as he took in her working appearance; the sleek hair, the fashionable make-up, the silk shirt and pleated wool skirt, classics given the look of the moment by being cinched by a Calvin Klein belt.

'Valissa! My word ... I'm not sure I should have known you if we'd passed in the street. You look stunning. Not that you didn't look equally stunning in Paxos, but in a completely different way'—extending his appraisal to her legs and feet.

As long as the weather remained mild, she was continuing to enjoy the freedom of not wearing tights. But no one would have guessed it. Her legs appeared to be clad in the finest mesh, and her black patent pumps with grosgrain bows were the kind which, with slight variations of toe and heel, were to be seen in Sloane Street every year not only on the feet of chic Londoners but worn by visiting Americans.

'The same could be said of you, Christopher,' she responded pleasantly, offering her hand. 'How long have you been back?'

'Long enough to have lost most of what little tan I did acquire. But you're a much better advertisement for holidays in the sun. I'm hoping I can persuade you to have lunch with me.'

'It's nice of you, but I never take more than twenty minutes for lunch. I have a sandwich and coffee at my desk.'

This was true. Except on rare occasions, such as when she had lunched with Elizabeth on her return, Valissa always preferred a quiet snack in the office to the lunch-time bustle of any of Knightsbridge's cheaper eating places.

'In that case, how about dinner?'

Valissa hesitated. She had a feeling that he intended to be persistent and, without any genuine excuses, it was going to be awkward to refuse.

'All right. Thank you.'

He produced an address book and a pen. 'If you'll give me your address, I'll pick you up about seven-thirty. Or is that too early?'

'No, that will be fine.'

Half an hour later, while she was eating her lunch

which that day consisted of cottage cheese and chutney
between slices of rye bread, Elizabeth looked in.

'I don't imagine Mr Carter came merely to say hello.
Did he succeed in dating you?'

'Yes . . . dinner this evening.'

'Splendid. Even if he didn't make much of an impression on you in Paxos, you can't continue to bury yourself
in work as you were doing before you went to Greece. To
grieve for Nick was one thing: to go into purdah again,
on account of a holiday romance which didn't work out,
would be something else,' said Elizabeth briskly.

From various remarks she had made since Valissa had
confided in her, it was clear that she visualised Dion as a
beautiful hunk of brawn, but with very little brain.

Valissa had not told her about his friendship with
Roderick who had said of him—*If I had a sister I should be
happy to see her married to Stefano.*

From her grandfather, with whom she had had several
telephone conversations since her return, she had discovered that the poet whom Dion had been quoting when
he spoke of 'the right true end of love' had been John
Donne.

Edward Cornford had put the phrase in context for her.

Whoever loves, if he do not propose
The right true end of love, he's one that goes
To sea for nothing but to make him sick.

Very apposite, Valissa thought bleakly, sipping black
coffee after Elizabeth had left her. Now, more than ever,
she regretted Dion's strange refusal to make love to her.
Perhaps if he had she would have regretted it, but not as
much as she regretted her present condition. To be almost
twenty-four years old, and to have loved twice yet still be
an unknowing virgin was indeed to have been to sea for
nothing.

If you change your mind, write to me, Dion had said. He
had given her an address in Athens from which mail was
forwarded to him, wherever he was.

Yet whenever she was tempted to change her mind, she
was surrounded by reminders of the difference between
her life in England and the life he had offered her in
Paxos.

However much she loved him, could she be happy without all the things which, here, she could take for granted?

Daily contact with interesting people. No language problem. Newspapers, magazines, books and even television, although the last was the least important as, being a selective viewer, she rarely watched more than one or two programmes a week.

The very wide range of food obtainable in London was something else she would miss. The solitary nature of her private life had made her into something of a gourmet. Whereas some people living alone couldn't be bothered to cook for themselves, Valissa's evening meal had become an enjoyable ritual depending partly on her own expertise in the kitchen, but also on the delicacies she was able to buy in small portions—one roast quail, a single slice of French pâté—from the Food Halls at Harrods.

However, much more important than any of these creature comforts was the telephone link with her grandfather, and the ease with which she could visit him every weekend. How could she leave him, at his age?

Her first dinner date with Christopher was enjoyable chiefly for the fact that it forced her to concentrate on him. While she was doing her duty as his guest, she could not think of Dion.

Christopher did not angle to be invited in when he took her home, nor did he kiss her goodnight. Evidently he was a slow worker, as perhaps was to be expected of a member of his profession.

When she refused a weekend date, explaining that she was going to see her grandfather, he offered to run her there in his car, and take himself for a walk while she was with the old man. But when she demurred, he did not press the suggestion.

'I'll call you next week,' were his parting words.

On Sunday, as soon as she drew back from embracing him, it seemed to Valissa that her grandfather had changed.

When he claimed to be feeling very fit, she hoped it was only her absence which made him appear more frail than she remembered, his movements slower and stiffer. Or perhaps it was that for two weeks she had been in the company of a man whose lithe, powerful body was still in the forefront of her mind.

Had her grandfather, also a tall man, ever walked with that long easy stride, ever swung Granny up in his arms? What would Dion be like in old age? She could visualise him with grizzled but still thick curls, and with many more lines on his face. But she couldn't imagine him shrinking, his straight body warping with age, his brown hands no longer warm and strong.

Looking at her grandfather, the line *And calm of mind, all passion spent* flashed into her mind. Where had it come from? Oh, yes, from Milton's *Samson Agonistes*, during her last year at school.

At the time the line had been merely something to be memorised. But now, looking at her grandfather's pale, wrinkled hand as he sampled the Metaxa brandy she had brought him, she understood *all passion spent*.

Perhaps he didn't mind being old because he had had a good life, surviving two wars and being very happy with Granny. Even now he still had his books, and lived in agreeable surroundings, solaced by many pleasant memories and only a few painful ones such as the loss of his only son.

But if she lived to be his age, what would she have to remember? What was worth remembering except love?

It was almost at the end of her visit that her grandfather said, 'My dear, I don't wish to pry into your affairs, but I feel there's something troubling you. Several times this afternoon you've become lost in thought, and your expression hasn't been happy. Is there any help I can give, or would you rather I minded my own business?'

Until he mentioned it, Valissa had not realised she had been noticeably distraite. Then, partly for his peace of mind and partly her own, she told him some of the truth—that, foolishly, she had lost her heart to an attractive Greek.

'But these holiday romances hardly ever come to anything, do they? I'll get over it,' she ended lightly. 'I also met quite a nice Englishman there, and I've had dinner with him since I've been back. So I'm not exactly pining away.'

'I see.' Mr Cornford offered no comment beyond saying, 'I'm glad he prevailed on you to dine with him. There's plenty of time for quiet evenings at home in one's later years. Don't waste your beauty, my dear child. You may not think so, as yet, but it's amazing how quickly the years slip away.'

On Monday, Eliot Rutherford reappeared, recharging the atmosphere in the building with the extra excitement of his presence. The business always ran smoothly, but the knowledge that he was in his studio on the top floor had a galvanic effect. His staff, habitually efficient—they didn't last if they were not—were stimulated to perform even more effectively.

During the morning the junior showroom assistant came up to Valissa's office with a florist's box.

Valissa opened the envelope taped to the lid. On the card inside was written *Christopher*. The flowers he had sent were two dozen dark red roses. It was an extravagant gesture which she wouldn't have expected of him.

That evening he rang up to ask her to go to the theatre with him on Friday. She agreed. She thanked him for the roses which were now in a vase on her coffee table.

He stayed on the line for some time and seemed reluctant to ring off. When he had, she wondered if it was unfair to go on seeing him.

On Tuesday, to her surprise, the post brought a letter addressed in her grandfather's distinctive handwriting, now rather more wavery than formerly.

He wrote that having pondered their conversation on Saturday, he wanted her to know that, should such a situation arise, he would be extremely disturbed if he felt that she had turned down an interesting post overseas, or an offer of marriage from a man who might want her to go abroad with him, on account of her affection for himself.

'Although less active nowadays, I have good health and a strong constitution, and expect to be alive for many years yet,' he had written. 'Moreover, I am not at all lonely, like many of my less fortunate contemporaries. I hope, therefore, that you will never feel obliged to refuse

any promising opportunity for success or happiness for my
benefit. Sacrifices of that nature are always a mistake, and
very often a burden to the people for whom they are made.'

He went on to describe an entertaining incident con-
cerning some fellow residents at the Hall and to add some
amusing snippets from a book he was reading, thereby
ending in a cheerful tone which supported the theme of
his letter.

By the end of November Valissa's face, hands and legs
had reverted to their natural colour. Only the parts of her
body protected by clothing still retained some of the tan
from her three weeks in Greece.

As the party season began Christopher, who had a large
circle of friends and acquaintances, would have taken her
out every night if she had been willing. But Valissa was
careful to keep a brake on their relationship, and to make
it clear that he was not the only man in her life.

In fact this was not a false impression. She did go out
with two other men during that period, and both lost no
time in making a pass at her. An unattached career girl of
her age must be a pushover, they seemed to think. Amused
at the thought of their amazement if they knew the truth
about her, Valissa corrected their theory.

She found that, since knowing Dion, she seemed to have
become unflappable where other men were concerned.
Or maybe it was merely that their techniques were so
anaemic compared with his.

You were adorable . . . everything a woman should be in a
man's arms . . . if I hadn't believed you were much younger we
should still be there, making love. Let's forget staying in Gaios for
supper. Let's go back to my place, or your place. I'm not hungry. I
only want you.

She remembered Dion's look and his tone as, barely
twenty-four hours after their first encounter, he had almost
swept her off her feet with his passionate warmth and
vitality.

In a way he was like Eliot: capable of making people
excel themselves, the difference between them being
that Eliot inspired his assistants to flights of imaginative
brilliance, and what Dion had kindled in her was an
upsurge of sensual awareness. Not for an instant

had either of the other two men made her feel that, locked in their arms, she would have a sublime experience. Dion had.

As December advanced, she recognised that although her increased social life helped to stop her from brooding, it was only a palliative. The moment she had nothing to distract her, she would find herself thinking of Dion, and wondering if he still missed her.

Choosing her Christmas cards, she debated sending one to him. But as he had made it very clear that his was an all-or-nothing attitude, in the end she decided against it.

About a week before Christmas she was spending her lunch break in Harrods, buying one or two last-minute presents, when a man turned away from a counter and knocked her arm with his elbow.

'I'm so sorry—clumsy of me. I hope I haven't hurt you?' he apologised.

'No, not at——*Roderick*!'

'Oh . . . hello. How are you?' he asked politely.

'You don't recognise me, do you? I'm Valissa Cornford. We met in Paxos. I was with Dion Stefanides . . . Stefano.'

'Yes, you had me foxed for a minute. You were dressed rather differently then, and your hair was longer, I believe.'

'It's still there, but pinned up.' She half-turned her head to show him the neat twists and coils. 'What a crush in here . . . and so hot. Freezing outside but sweltering in here.'

'Mm, pretty near suffocation point. Not my scene at all. Look, why don't we both cut and run . . . have a quiet drink somewhere to restore us?'

As soon as she murmured, 'All right', he began to steer her through the press of shoppers towards the nearest exit.

He took her to the bar of a nearby hotel where, if it wasn't precisely quiet, it was peaceful compared with the hurly-burly in the store.

'I suppose, running into me here, you might guess that Dion and I——that we broke it off,' said Valissa, after he had ordered drinks. 'Or did you already know that? I don't know how much contact you have with him.'

'It depends. You could say we keep in touch on a spas-
modic basis. As it happens I ran into him about ten days
ago—not here, in the south of France. I was spending a
few days with my godmother in Monte Carlo, and he
happened to be there . . . on a boat in the harbour,' he
added explanatorily.

'I see. And he told you what had happened?'

'He didn't say much. Merely that it hadn't worked out.
Pity. I'd never seen him looking as happy as he was that
night in Paxos. He was like a kid in love for the first time.
Maybe it *was* the first time he'd ever really lost his heart
to a girl. Any guy with Stefano's . . . charisma has plenty
of offers of the other thing, but not too much chance of
finding good old-fashioned, till death do us part, life-long
love.'

His eyes were cold as he took in her London chic; the
bulky yet featherweight jacket of reversible violet-blue
mohair, thrown open to show a dark violet silk shirt with
a quilted yoke and cuffs, and a pale grey suede skirt with
matching boots. Real amethysts, left to her by her grandmother and re-set in a silver pendant of her own design,
flashed purple fire on her breast and winked from the
lobes of her ears.

'But maybe that wasn't what you wanted,' Roderick
finished, with a shrug.

'It was exactly what I wanted, but there were too many
obstacles. Love isn't always plain sailing. I should have
thought you would have understood that, Roderick.
Stefano told me a little about your own problems. I hope
they have a happier outcome than ours did.'

Suddenly, just as the waiter came back with their
drinks, tears brimmed in her eyes and her lower lip started
to tremble.

As she fumbled in her bag for a handkerchief, Roderick
thrust a large folded one into her hand. She pressed it
hard against her mouth and took a tight grip on herself.
By the time the waiter had gone, she was in control
again.

'So you were and still are in love with him,' he said
quietly, handing her gin and tonic to her. 'Then why the
devil did you pull out of it?'

'Mainly because I have a very old grandfather who isn't dependent on me, and who says he wouldn't miss me. But if he were ill, I couldn't bear not to be with him—he's been my father as well as my grandfather— and as Dion's wife I shouldn't be able to fly here and back whenever I wanted to. There are other reasons as well,' she added honestly.

'This is the real me, Roderick. Not the outdoor girl you saw in Paxos. Oh, I loved the island and its peace; but not for every day of my life, particularly when the weather is bad there. Books and music and art galleries mean a great deal to me, and——'

'Stefano isn't a complete hick, you know,' he cut in.

'No, I know. He's amazingly well read. But he won't even consider coming to England, and I couldn't be happy in Paxos. For a year or two, perhaps. Not for ever. Not even with Dion.'

Roderick drank some gin and looked thoughtful. 'I take your point,' he said, at length. 'Yes, that island is strictly a summer place—unless anyone had the means to build a luxury house there, with maybe a helicopter pad to make it a ten-minute hop to the nearest airport instead of three hours on the ferry.'

'For a Greek, such as Aristotle Onassis, with an un-imaginable fortune, there are never any problems,' she said dryly.

'No practical problems. Money—even millions of it— doesn't obviate all life's difficulties,' he corrected her.

'No, I suppose not,' she conceded.

No doubt he was thinking of the powerful sense of duty to one's heritage which Dion had said was the obstacle between Roderick and his equally tradition-bound baroness.

'Do you think that, in time, you'll get over him?' he asked her.

'This time, I think not,' she said sadly. 'Years ago I was engaged to someone who was killed. I did get over that, eventually. Although I didn't know I had until I met Dion. How can I "get over" him when he's still there . . . somewhere . . . and perhaps still wants me? On his terms.'

'I'm sure he still wants you,' said Roderick. 'But yes, it would always have to be on his terms. He's that kind of man. He's also the kind who, whatever impossible thing his wife had set her heart on, would do his damnedest to get it for her—and probably succeed.'

He paused. 'You say this is the real you, Valissa'—with a gesture encompassing her, and the Christmas issue of *Vogue*, and the green-wrapped, gold-printed Harrods parcels which were lying on the sofa beside her. He leaned towards her, a slightly self-mocking smile superimposing on seriousness. 'I wouldn't admit it to everyone, but I think a man without a woman, or a woman without a man, is incomplete . . . half a person.'

'I think so, too. *I know it*,' she added, in an anguished whisper. 'Oh, Roderick, I wish I hadn't run into you. I was trying not to think about Dion, but now, talking about him . . .' She left the sentence unfinished and reached for her glass, her hand trembling slightly as she lifted it to her lips. 'What sort of boat was he on? How long was he going to be there? Did you see much of him?'

'We had a meal together. The yacht left the following morning. Compared with her, my boat's a dinghy. She was one of the floating palaces you see in places like Monte. Her owner is one of the richest men in Europe.'

'Oh, really?' she said, without interest. Fabulous yachts and great wealth had never been among her daydreams. 'I must go—I have work waiting for me. Thank you for the drink.'

As she rose, and Roderick rose with her, she asked, 'Is there any hope that the complications in your life may resolve themselves more happily than ours?'

'Not immediately. But at least Lucia and I see each other frequently, and I have a pied-à-terre here where we stay together from time to time. She's arriving later today, as a matter of fact. I think her longing for children will win her over eventually.'

'So you, too, mean to have it your way,' Valissa remarked, her mouth wry.

'Isn't that the way women want it?' was his unruffled answer.

For the rest of the day, she did little work, her ability

to concentrate upset by the unexpected encounter.

That night she had dinner with Christopher who tried
to persuade her to spend the Christmas holiday, or part of
it, with him at his parents' home.

'You're entitled to some fun,' he persisted, when she
refused. 'Why not come to us for Boxing Day?'

'It's kind of you, Christopher, but I'd rather spend the
whole time with Grandpa. It might be our last Christmas
together, and the Hall is a lovely place for it. The Warden
and his wife decorate a huge tree, and hang lots of holly
everywhere. Other people besides Grandpa have guests.
In fact the local pub, which does bed and breakfast and
where I stay, is booked up from year to year by people
with relations at the Hall. There's no question of my being
the only youngish person around. There'll be children,
teenagers, all ages. Last year, while Grandpa was snooz-
ing, I went for an afternoon tramp with an actor whose
mother lives there. It was anything but dull, I assure
you.'

'What about the New Year? Can you come to us then?'
Christopher suggested. 'I'd like you to meet my parents.'

What he meant, she suspected, was that he wanted to
show her to his parents, and see what they thought of her
before committing himself to a closer relationship. Not a
man of swift, bold decisions, Christopher Carter.

On Christmas Eve, she and old Mr Cornford went to
the midnight service in the parish church. There was a
path direct from the Hall to the gate of the churchyard.
Warmly wrapped against the frosty night, they walked
slowly along it, arm-in-arm, and afterwards slowly back
again, to drink toddy by the log fire in the oak-panelled
entrance hall.

Then a couple staying at the pub gave Valissa a lift to
the village, and soon she was climbing into her bed which
the landlord's wife had warmed for her with an old-
fashioned earthenware bottle with a fleecy cover.

It would have been a perfect Christmas—if only Dion
had been there to share it with them. She wondered where
he was spending the festival. Perhaps still on board the
floating palace where no doubt the crew enjoyed fare not
greatly inferior to that of the millionaire owner.

January and February seemed endless. After a heavy cold had disrupted her social life for a week, deliberately she let it lapse, making her work an excuse to refuse engagements, as she had in the past, before Paxos.

In March, Edward Cornford died in his sleep, leaving his affairs in perfect order with instructions that he wished to be cremated and his ashes not to be preserved.

'My books will be my memorial,' he had written, in a letter for his granddaughter to read after his death. 'Keep them or dispose of them, as you choose. Books survive for a long time. I like to think that perhaps, a century or two from now, some of mine will be read and enjoyed, and my book-plate will be a better reminder of my existence than an overgrown grave and a weathered headstone.'

For two weeks Valissa was oppressed by the loneliness of having no one left alive who belonged to her. Friends, however close, were not the same as relations. In some cases, they might be preferable. But not when the relations had been loved and valued.

Only gradually did she realise that the other side of the coin was freedom. She no longer had any ties. Even her job wasn't essential any more. Her grandfather had left her everything. Not in London, but in many less expensive places, she could get along without working. Not for ever maybe, but certainly for the time being.

The acceptance that her love for Dion was the paramount force in her life, and that now she could go to him without deserting her grandfather, came to her one night in her flat. The next morning, as soon as she reached the office, she asked Eliot's secretary to arrange for her to discuss something personal with him as soon as possible.

It happened that the designer had time to spare for her later that day.

'What's the problem, Valissa?' he asked her, as she entered his studio and he gestured for her to sit down.

There was never any preliminary chit-chat with Eliot. He always came straight to the point, and no detail escaped him. Before she reached the chair he indicated, he had taken in everything she was wearing. Had she changed the strap on her watch, he would have noticed it.

'I want to give you a month's notice.' Forestalling the
inevitable question, she went on, 'When I was in Greece
in September, someone asked me to marry him. I thought
it wouldn't work, but since then I've changed my mind.
Now I'm sure it will.'

Her employer gazed at her in silence for about fifteen
seconds. He was not married himself, but neither was he
known to be homosexual. Elizabeth said he was a neuter
whose only passion was for his métier.

He began to fire questions at her. The name of the
man? His occupation? Had he been to England to see
her? Had they corresponded?

Valissa was rather amused by this stringent interroga-
tion. His curiosity surprised her, but she did not mind
answering his questions.

However, when he said, 'You must be mad,' her soft
lips compressed. She stopped leaning back in the chair
and sat up very straight.

But she kept her tone mild as she answered; 'I wasn't
canvassing your opinion, merely giving you notice.'

'You're going to get my opinion. You're too valuable a
member of my team to be allowed to throw up your career
for a Greek you met six months ago and haven't seen
since.'

For five minutes Eliot harangued her, repeating all the
objections she had seen for herself at the outset. Now,
after half a year of being, as Roderick had put it, an
incomplete person, she knew that a life without love was
far more barren than a life without art, music and litera-
ture.

When, finally, she was able to get a word in edgeways,
she said, 'I appreciate that you mean well, Eliot, but this
is no crazy impulse. I've had plenty of time to think it
over, and my mind is made up—unshakeably. I shall
leave here four weeks from today. I know how busy you
are. I won't keep you any longer.'

That evening she started writing a letter to Dion. It
was difficult to find the right words. Although she hated
to admit it, Eliot had sown a doubt in her mind.
Supposing Dion no longer wanted her?

He had in December, according to Roderick. But now

it was March, nearly April. A lot could have happened since the turn of the year.

Also, if she wrote to him care of the address in Athens, it might be a long time before the letter reached him. She would have to wait for a reply not knowing if the letter hadn't yet arrived at wherever he was, or if he was putting off replying because he had found someone else.

I need to meet him in person to know if he still cares for me, she thought. But how, when I don't know where to find him?

Maybe Roderick would know. She asked Directory Enquiries for his telephone number. But the voice which answered her call to his home said that Sir Roderick was in the West Indies, soon to take part in a week of sailing races off Antigua. He would not be back until late May.

Valissa began to think that, instead of giving notice immediately, she should have asked for a week off and flown to Athens, and from there to wherever Dion was to be found.

The excitement of her life-changing decision, and the fear that it might yet be frustrated, kept her awake half the night.

If the cottage had one large room added to it, she could keep all her grandfather's furniture and books as well as her own possessions. But how much would it cost to have them transported to Paxos? Too much, perhaps.

Plans, ideas and questions seethed in her restless mind.

Strangely, in the morning she wasn't tired. For the first time in months she felt happy and full of vitality. The problem of tracing Dion was still unsolved, but nevertheless she walked to work with a light step, and a feeling of spring in the air although showers and sleet had been forecast on the radio.

Soon after she had started work, Elizabeth, who had been out of the office the previous day, came to see her.

'Eliot rang me up last night in no end of a tizz. He's inclined to blame me for okaying that extra week's holiday. You should be flattered he's so fussed. I shall miss you, Valissa.'

'*You* don't think I've gone crazy, then?'

'I think it was crazier to become an unofficial nun as

you were before you went on that trip. On your sanity at
the moment I wouldn't like to give an opinion without
seeing this Greek god of yours.'

'I'm sorry Eliot is peeved with you. That's unfair.
I——'

She broke off as the intercom bleeped. When she flipped
the switch, Eliot's voice commanded her presence immediately.

'Oh, dear, not another tirade!' Valissa sighed, rolling
her eyes.

'Bear up. He can rant, but he can't actually stop you,'
Elizabeth reminded her.

However, as soon as she entered his studio, Valissa
could see that Eliot was no longer in the irascible mood
in which she had left him the day before.

He smiled at her. 'Good morning, Valissa. What's that
you're wearing round your neck?'

She unfastened the silver chain and handed the object
to him. 'It's a silver bodkin which my grandfather used to
use as a bookmark.'

He picked up a magnifying glass to examine more
closely the blunt-ended sliver of silver with a hole and a
slot at each end of it.

'Not hallmarked, I see, but it has some initials scrat-
ched on it.'

'Yes, it may have been a courtship present. For several
centuries people of both sexes used bodkins for threading
drawstrings and ribbons in their clothes.'

He handed it back to her. 'Interesting.' He sat down
and picked up a letter which had been lying on his blotter.
'This commission came in this morning. Does the name
John Roxburgh mean anything to you?'

She shook her head. 'Should it?'

'It's a name well known among financiers, but he
doesn't attract much attention from the gossip columnists.
He's the son of Quentin Roxburgh who founded the fortune just after the Second World War when I was laun-
ching my own career. The father married a Greek girl. I
suppose she was a daughter of one of the shipping
magnates, and that helped him make his first million. But
the son is worth five times as much.'

'What does he want us to do for him?' she asked, wondering if Eliot was trying to involve her in a job which would take months to complete.

'I thought you might already know that.'

'I don't think I've even heard of the man,' she said perplexedly.

'He's heard of you. From a Mrs Irving K. Portland of Houston, Texas.'

For some moments the name meant nothing. Then she remembered the American charter party on Roderick's yacht.

'But I hardly know Mrs Portland. I only met her once, quite briefly.'

'You must have told her you worked for me, and she knew my reputation, as most rich American women do,' he added blandly. 'Presumably her husband is a friend of Roxburgh. I seem to recall that he's unmarried. No doubt in matters of this nature he takes advice from the wives of his friends and associates.'

He referred to the letter in his hand. 'He's built himself a holiday house on land inherited from his mother's side of the family. The structure won't be completed until late May, but meanwhile he wants the interior designed and the garden landscaped. As he knows you are one of my underlings, he wants you on site a fortnight today to cope with the preliminaries. He'll be passing through London several times during May. I'll see him then, when the visuals and sample boards are ready.'

'He takes a great deal for granted,' Valissa said dryly. 'You might not have had an underling free in a fortnight.'

She had smiled inwardly at his choice of word, knowing it was intended to correct any uppishness engendered by having her name mentioned by a prospective client.

Although Eliot's contribution to most schemes consisted of one or two changes of detail to visuals prepared by his staff, he was not inclined to share any kudos. Why should he? His alterations often made the difference between an excellent interior design and a brilliant one.

'A multi-millionaire can take most things for granted,' he retorted. 'He doesn't, you'll be pleased to hear, expect us to invent a background for him. He enclosed a page of notes on his tastes and the possessions he proposes to install in the house. Like me, he pays great attention to detail— or rather instructs his secretary to do so. The letter tells you what flight to take and everything else you need to know about the journey. I won't give you the originals. Collect the photo-copies from Jane on your way down-stairs.'

'But, Eliot, this job is going to take far more than a month if you expect me to carry it through as well as handling preliminaries.'

'Yes, Roxburgh wants the place finished by the end of August and, even with his resources behind, you'll have your work cut out.'

'You seem to forget that yesterday I gave you a month's notice.'

Eliot's smile had a palpable smugness.

'Forgetfulness is not one of my characteristics. *You* have forgotten to ask where John Roxburgh is building his house. It happens to be in the Ionian Sea . . . on the island of Paxos, to be precise. So you will be reunited with your heart-throb rather sooner than you anticipated. And, I hope, after spending much of the summer in his company, by the time this commission is completed, you'll have thought better of marrying him.'

CHAPTER SEVEN

'Paxos!' Valissa ejaculated. 'But it's not a millionaire's island. What on earth is he doing building there, of all places?'

'Skorpios was not a millionaire's island until Aristotle Onassis bought it.'

'I thought Skorpios was in the Aegean where the good weather lasts all year round.'

'No, Skorpios is close to Lefkas, some way south of Paxos,' said Eliot. 'I doubt if a man of Roxburgh's calibre ever indulges a whim unless it's also a good investment. Off you go, Valissa.'

Dazed by this turn of events, she would have neglected to collect the photo-copies from his secretary if Jane had not seen her passing and called to her.

Before going back to her own room, Valissa looked in on Elizabeth.

'Maybe there is something in Fate,' was the older woman's reaction, on being told of the Roxburgh commission. 'It could be that you and your Greek can find a niche for yourself in John Roxburgh's entourage,' she went on thoughtfully. 'He'll be bound to want caretakers, won't he? You could find yourself with the run of his place, and only living in the cottage for the two or three weeks a year when he and his guests are in residence.'

'I think that's rather hopeful, but the mere fact of his presence must improve the amenities on the island,' said Valissa.

'Or spoil it.'

'I don't see why. He isn't the kind of millionaire whose every move attracts publicity. Eliot thinks he's a bachelor. I wonder why he isn't married?'

'Prefers a succession of "friends", I expect. As far as your marriage plans are concerned, this does give you a chance to take another long look at each other, and to be really sure you're suited.'

'Dion may not be there now. In December, I heard he was working on a yacht in the south of France. My only contact with him is an address in Athens.'

'Then write to him there, telling him you'll be in Paxos all summer, on and off. I'm sure it won't be long before he shows up.'

Presently, alone in her office, Valissa read Mr Roxburgh's letter to Eliot, and then studied the accompanying notes.

He sounded an ideal client, firm in certain likes and dislikes but otherwise open-minded. The list of belongings which he wanted to be set off sounded very exciting.

He owned several of the Ming jade water buffaloes which rich Chinese had stroked as an aid to digestion, a jade horse's head of the Han dynasty, and a T'ang camel. Evidently all his Chinese pieces were from the simple, forceful period preferred by connoisseurs and not the over-elaborate objects made when Chinese art was degenerating.

A Greek bronze deer and a Spanish Madonna sounded as if they had great decorative possibilities, as did his collection of icons and of rugs made by South Persian nomads, all with lions as their principal motif.

The last object on the list was a Roman bronze copy of a Greek figure of Dionysios, the original having been made in the third century before Christ.

Valissa wondered if his Dionysios looked anything like hers—if indeed he was still hers.

That evening she rang her illustrator friend, Andrew, who had lent her the apartment at Loggos. She asked if it was vacant at present.

'Yes, sure. Do you want to use it again?'

'If I can swing a week's holiday. What with the weather this year, and losing my grandfather, I feel I could do with a break.'

'The weather there now won't be like it was in September, but it's sure to be better than here. If you're tough, you might even swim,' he said.

The next day she told Eliot she would like to go to Paxos a week before Mr Roxburgh wanted her to start work.

'By all means. I have no objection—in fact it's a good idea. You can have a scout round before he arrives, and impress him with your rapid grasp. I rely on you to handle him well. If he's satisfied this time, he'll use us again in the future, and bring other clients in his wake. It's an important assignment, Valissa, the most important you've ever had. But I'm confident you can deal with it. As long as you remember that, after next week, you'll be there to work. Romance must take second place.'

'I'll remember it,' she assured him. 'But don't expect me back when the work is completed, Eliot. I meant what I said the other day. I'm serious about my Greek. It doesn't matter that he hasn't a steady job now that I have a small independence. I shan't sell the flat for the time being, but I'm making arrangements to let it.'

'You'll change your mind when you see him again. You'll wonder what you saw in the fellow. These holiday affairs never last, my dear girl,' he said shortly.

'Perhaps one day you may meet him, and then you'll know what I saw in him,' she answered serenely.

That night she wrote to Dion, reminding him of Irving and Lillian Portland, and explaining that, because of Lillian's advice to a financier called John Roxburgh, she was being sent to Paxos by Eliot, and would be on the island for the greater part of the summer.

Our client has arranged for me to put up at the Paxos Beach Hotel until the building work is finished, after which I can stay at the house with someone from the nearest village coming in to clean, she wrote. *I don't know yet where the house is. Perhaps on the west coast. He mentions a swimming pool, which would seem unnecessary near the east coast with all those gorgeous bays. However, I'm sure such a luxurious place must be the subject of much interest and gossip, so you will soon find out where I am if you are also in Paxos this summer.*

I ran into Roderick before Christmas, and he told me you had a job on a 'floating palace', so perhaps you won't be coming home for some time. If you are there, I should like to see you. Yours— Valissa.

Yours. It could mean so much or so little. At the bottom

of an informal business letter it meant nothing. At the
bottom of this letter it was meant literally. She was his;
body, heart and soul. But he wouldn't guess that from the
rest of the letter which was no more than friendly in its
tone. Perhaps it was too noncommittal. Maybe she ought
to put Love, another word which could be used casually.

In the end she decided to leave the ending as it stood.
She had already checked the airmail postage to Greece.
Having sealed and stamped the envelope, she went out
and posted it immediately, so as not to be plagued by
second thoughts.

The first time she had landed at Loggos, Anna had been
on the quay looking out for her. This time, arriving without warning, she had to go to Anna's house for the key.

'Thespinis Cornford! Oh. . . .' An explosion of Greek
followed Anna's startled exclamation at the sight of her.

Although the apartment smelt fresh, as if it had been
aired recently, the floor and the tables were dusty, for
which the Greek woman apologised.

Valissa dredged her memory for what little Greek she
had learnt on her previous visit, and came up with '*Then
pirazi*' which she hoped meant 'It doesn't matter.'

She signalled that she was hungry, and would have an
early supper at one of the tavernas, at which Anna
nodded approvingly and shook her head in disapproval of
Valissa's loss of weight and the hollowness of her cheeks.

She also made gestures to show that the floor would be
swept and the bed made up by the time Valissa came
back.

It was pleasant to be remembered, and greeted like an
old friend, by the owner of the taverna and his wife.

She ate a substantial meal of soup, moussaka and an
ice, and drank two glasses of wine, paying for the bottle
and taking it back to the apartment with her. Then she
sat outside on the terrace, sipping more wine and thinking.
She was still wearing the pants she had travelled in, and
her mohair jacket, so she wasn't cold sitting out there.
But the spring night was very much cooler than the evening in late September when she and Dion had parted, as
she thought, forever.

Next morning she overslept, and was woken by Anna using her pass-key to come in with a basket of provisions for Valissa's breakfast—coffee, milk, honey, butter and fresh bread.

In the nine o'clock sun it was warm enough to eat outside with bare legs and rolled up sleeves. Her mouth full of bread and honey, Valissa leaned on the rail, looking down at the sparkling harbour. In London, probably, it was pouring.

Later she arranged for the taxi from Lakka to collect her and take her to Gaios. The driver dropped her by the war memorial in the *platia*. She debated having a drink in one of the cafés, and decided to stroll around first. There were more people about than she had expected to see. Then she remembered being told that the villas with yellow placards on their gates, which were let by an agency called the Greek Islands Club, came into use early in April.

A sight attracting quite a few bystanders was a magnificent yacht moored near where the ferries berthed. She was out of Piraeus, the port of Athens, and her name was written in Greek letters with the English version underneath: *Selene*.

Valissa paused at the rear of the people admiring her.

'How much do you reckon a boat of that size would cost, Harry?' a Yorkshirewoman asked her husband.

'A couple of million at least, love. Maybe three million even,' he answered. 'Must have a mint of money, whoever owns it.'

As he spoke, a member of the crew, with the name of the vessel printed in blue on his white sweat shirt, came down the accommodation ladder. He was followed by a man in a plain shirt.

Valissa gasped. It was Dion. This must be the 'floating palace' mentioned by Roderick.

Ignoring their audience, the two men went in different directions, Dion towards the *platia*.

Swiftly Valissa followed, her heart beating fast with excitement.

At the corner of the square, she said loudly, '*Kalimera, Kyrie Dionysios*.'

'Valissa!' He looked as startled as she had been.

Time froze as they gazed at each other. Only vaguely was she aware of a high-pitched shriek in the distance. All her senses were focussed on Dion whose grey eyes were suddenly blazing with the look she remembered so well. The look which told her she was beautiful, and that he loved her.

A child was tugging at his arm. 'Uncle Dion, come quickly! Carey's knocked all his teeth out.'

Loud howls from the far side of the *platia* confirmed that an accident had happened.

'That damned kid——' Dion said furiously.

Leaving Valissa still rooted, he sprinted in the direction of the cries accompanied by the little girl whose pronunciation of Dion had made it sound more like John.

Before she had pulled herself together, he was running back towards her, a smaller child in his arms, its face a mask of blood.

'I told him he shouldn't ride it so fast, Uncle Dion. But he wouldn't listen,' the little girl panted, hurrying alongside with the bicycle. Again, she made the D sound like a J.

'Stay there. I shan't be long,' he told Valissa, as they passed her.

'What happened to the child, Miss Cornford?' a voice enquired from behind her, after she had turned to watch him springing back up the ladder he had so recently descended.

Valissa found that a couple named Brentforth, to whom she had chatted on the ferry, had strolled up beside her.

'He fell off the bicycle,' she told them.

'It may not be much,' said Mrs Brentforth in the placid tone of a woman who had brought up three boisterous sons. 'The blood was probably mostly from his nose. He was making a lot of noise for a child who'd been seriously hurt.'

Valissa said, 'I heard the other child say he'd knocked all his teeth out. But perhaps she was exaggerating.'

'Pity I'm not a doctor, I could offer my services. I'd like to go on board that yacht. She's magnificent, isn't she?' said Mr Brentforth.

Valissa nodded.

'Her owner is English, rather surprisingly,' he went on. 'In these days of high taxation, there are not many Englishmen left who can afford to run a yacht of that size.'

'Are you sure? She has a Greek name, and her port of registration is Greek.'

'He's only half English, Peter,' his wife put in. She turned to Valissa. 'His mother was Greek. He's building a beautiful house here. Some people we met in a café last night after dinner told us about it. If you take a boat up the coast to that place where you got off, Miss Cornford, you'll see it on a headland above a lovely bay. Peter and I didn't see it last night because after you'd landed we went and sat in the saloon. You'd think with that beautiful yacht he wouldn't need a house as well. What it is to be a millionaire.'

'Did they tell you his name? Was it Roxburgh?'

'Yes, that's right. How did you know? Have you heard of him? I can't say we have.'

'Yes, I've heard of him.'

'Come on, Molly, we'd better post those cards. If you don't do it on the first day, very often you get home before the cards do,' said Mr Brentforth, with a chuckle. 'See you later, I expect, Miss Cornford.'

'Yes, I expect so,' she answered abstractedly.

The discovery that Mr Roxburgh's land, inherited from his mother's family, was on the same side of Paxos as the cottage of Dion's grandparents puzzled her. How odd, Dion never mentioning that a half-Greek English millionaire owned a stretch of that coast.

She saw him returning down the ladder, his white shirt spattered with blood. If she hadn't known what his name was, she would have thought the child had called him Uncle John . . .

An idea, so wild as to seem impossible, came into her mind with the impact of a physical blow. Mentally reeling, she waited for him to reach her.

Automatically, she asked, 'Is the little boy all right?'

'Yes, yes . . . his own fault, little wretch . . . what are you doing here?' He took her by the arm and propelled her away from the waterfront, towards the rear of the *platia*. 'Your letter said next week, not this week.'

'You've received my letter already?'

She wouldn't have thought there had been time for it to reach Athens and the yacht to come from there to Paxos. But perhaps, by the Corinth Canal, it wasn't as far as she imagined.

Dion said, 'The yacht has a radio-telephone. I called Athens yesterday and was told there was a letter from London. I told my . . . aunt to read it to me, in case it was anything urgent.' His tone was curt and displeased.

They all fell into place, all the things which had seemed slightly odd while he was pretending to be Dion but were easily explained now that she had uncovered his true identity.

'Your aunt . . . or your private secretary . . . Mr Roxburgh?' she asked, resisting his hold on her arm and coming to a standstill.

His expression became a blank mask. 'What are you talking about?'

'I think you've been making a fool of me. You aren't really a . . . a jack-of-all-trades called Dionysios Stefanides. You're John Roxburgh, the man who wrote to Eliot and had me sent out here. It's no use denying it. I heard the child call you Uncle John, and immediately afterwards someone told me who the yacht belonged to.'

His hand dropped from her arm, but for several moments he said nothing, his expression unreadable still.

At last, he said, 'My full name is John Dionysios Stefanides Roxburgh. The Greek form of John is Yannis. I was always called Dion here. Why did you come a week early, instead of following the instructions?'

'I wanted a rest beforehand . . . before starting work for Eliot's important new client.'

'That's unfortunate,' was his clipped comment. 'Very unfortunate. However, as you are here, you'd better come on board and have lunch. I have my sister and her husband and four other people staying with me. They're here for another two days. Only my alter ego, Dion Stefanides, was remaining in Paxos when *Selene* went back to Athens. He would have met you next week with the news that Mr

Roxburgh had been detained, and you were required to work from the brief you'd been given.'

'But why?—*Why* this elaborate deception to keep me from knowing who you really were?'

'Because——'

'My dear John, why the bloodied shirt? And who is this pretty young woman I haven't met yet?' a drawling voice interrupted.

A man in a pink shirt and curly-brimmed shady straw hat was strolling towards them. As Valissa looked at him, he removed the hat with a sweeping gesture. He had thick silver hair, somewhat long.

'Valissa, this is Prosper Arnold whose very fine portrait of my mother enhanced his reputation as a painter of beautiful women, but whose present subject is unlikely to add to his stature,' Dion said sardonically. 'Miss Cornford is here to design the interior of my house, Prosper. You will have the pleasure of sitting next to her at lunch. The blood is Carey's. He fell off his bike. If you'll bring Valissa aboard, I'll go ahead and get changed.'

They were still shaking hands as he strode away.

'As perhaps you've gathered from that remark, my present—most reluctant—sitter is John,' the artist told her, with a smile. 'His is an interesting face, don't you think? Although he doesn't see it as such.'

'I think it's a wonderful face,' she agreed, shaken out of her normal reserve by the shocks of the past ten minutes.

He looked at her rather searchingly. 'You've known him some time?'

'I met him here, last September. Have you been to Paxos before, Mr Arnold?'

'Prosper . . . please. There's no formality on *Selene*. No, I haven't. A charming place, from what I've seen of it.'

'Yes. Was Mrs Roxburgh's name Selene?'

'No, she was called Loukia. Selene means "mistress of the moon". She was the original moon goddess usurped by Artemis, the huntress. She, when she had finished driving her moon chariot, spent the rest of the night in the woods with her silver bow, shooting at animals and any unlucky human huntsmen who happened to catch her engaged in what my daughters call skinny-dipping.

In the same way Apollo, her twin brother, usurped the original sun god, Helios.'

They were now at the foot of the accommodation ladder, and he gestured for her to precede him.

Before she saw Dion again—she knew he would always be Dion to her—Valissa had met his brother-in-law, Marcus, Prosper's wife Davina, and the two other guests, Werner and Romy Merz, both of whom spoke perfect English. Marcus's wife was still attending to her small son.

From the moment he reappeared, it seemed to Valissa that when Dion had referred to his alter ego it had not been merely an expression but a literal truth. Suddenly he was a different man; an urbane and amusing host, but with a coldness in his eyes, a glint of steel which had never been there before.

Gone, too, were the faded jeans of September. Now he wore pale sand-coloured pants, a light V-necked cashmere sweater, and a shirt with a silk scarf knotted casually inside the open collar.

The reason for the sweater was apparent later, when they had lunch at sea, the yacht having left the harbour while they were drinking aperitifs. Fortunately Valissa had bought a velour top with her, or she might have been a little chilly. With a top on the breeze was pleasant as they sat round a table on deck, waited on by two uniformed stewards.

Valissa sat between Werner and Prosper, and near to Dion's sister, Gaia, who was several years older than he. The children had their lunch elsewhere, in the charge of an au pair who should have been keeping an eye on them at the time of the accident.

Mrs Brentforth's surmise had been correct; it had not been a serious tumble, and the only tooth lost had been an already wobbly milk tooth.

Before they had finished the first course, a choice of several sorts of pâté with hot bread and salad, the yacht was once more at anchor.

Valissa, who was sitting with her back to the coast, forcing herself to attend to the conversation and not to steal glances at their host, was unaware of this until

Prosper remarked, 'There you are, my dear. There's your bare canvas, as it were.'

She turned in the direction he indicated. To port lay the stretch of coast her first glimpse of which had been from a dinghy in a downpour of rain. Now, on the once bare headland, stood a large, rambling building, its walls faced with weathered stone, its roofs clad with reclaimed tiles so that it looked not new but as if it had stood there for decades. Two arches with bells suspended in them reinforced the impression that it could once have been a small monastery.

'It's beautiful,' she exclaimed softly. Impulsively she swung to face the man it belonged to. 'Oh, Dion, it's perfect!'

'I'm glad you approve.'

His words and his tone were pleasant enough, but his eyes were derisive, quenching her spontaneous delight so that, baffled and hurt, she looked at Prosper as she said, 'I—I thought it might be very modern. I find this more ... sympathetic.'

'And I, too,' agreed the older man. 'It's very well done, and the conception is John's. I tell him he should have been an architect.'

'You call John "Dion", I notice,' remarked his sister, as the stewards began to serve devilled poussins with brown rice and purple broccoli.

'You're privileged,' Gaia went on. 'Only my mother and her relations used to call my brother by his Greek name. When he first went away to school with J.D.S. Roxburgh on his trunk, the other boys tried to find out what the D and S stood for. I remember how upset my mother was when he came home on his first *exeat* with a puffed-up eye and masses of bruises from the fights he'd had over those initials.'

'I knew better than to let on what they stood for. African, Indian and Arab names were taken for granted, but an Ancient Greek name—I think not,' said Dion, speaking to Romy and Davina who were seated on either side of him. 'I preferred a few black eyes to ten years of being the butt of schoolboy jokes, not only about my names but probably about the sexual customs of the

Ancient Greeks as well,' he added sardonically.

'I'd have thought you'd have been too big to be bullied or teased, John,' said Davina.

'Not at eight. I hadn't shot up then.'

'You were sent to school at eight?' exclaimed Romy. 'I think that's too young for a child to leave home.'

'So do I. I don't want Carey to go away at all,' said Gaia, with a glance at her husband which suggested that this was a bone of contention between them. 'But my father and mother had a strange kind of battle over us, although more over John than myself. Father wanted him to grow up a thoroughbred Englishman, and boarding school at eight was with that object. My mother wanted him to be Greek, hence the frequent holidays here which Father couldn't forbid because he had promised to let her come back whenever she wished. Anyway, he was too engrossed in his business affairs to have very much time for family life.'

'And which do you feel yourself to be now? English or Greek?' asked Davina.

'I'm totally English,' said Gaia. 'I take after Father in looks. The only Greek thing about me is my name.'

'And you, John?'

'I regard myself as a mongrel which, being an internationalist politically, I am very happy to be,' he answered.

This led to a political discussion which lasted until the end of the meal at which time Dion suggested that, after their coffee, they might like a closer look at his house.

The day before, it appeared, the yacht had anchored off the west coast in order for his guests to explore the caves. Before that, they had been circling Corfu.

Selene's tender was a launch large enough to take all six of them, the two children and the au pair, and the seaman in charge.

The landing-stage where Dion had helped Valissa ashore before carrying her up to the cottage had been enlarged and improved. An electrically-operated hoist, which would be concealed among shrubs, was being engineered on the hillside to carry supplies up to the house, and give lifts to guests who found the climb up beyond them. Although this had now been made easier by the building of a wide stone staircase with pavilioned landings at each of the turns.

'In time, these will be covered with creepers,' Dion explained, on the way up.

'Won't the water shortage on the island preclude you from having much of a garden? How will you irrigate?' asked Marcus.

'No problem. It's a matter of building adequate catchments. All the Ionian islands have a much higher winter rainfall than most of Greece. Paxos has an annual fall of over a hundred centimetres, which is more than in some parts of England,' replied his brother-in-law.

His answer reminded Valissa of Eliot's remark that a man like John Roxburgh would never indulge a whim unless it was also a good investment. Yet as they entered the house and she saw that the rooms within were as gracious in conception as the exterior, she felt sure that his reason for building the place was the realisation of a dream and had nothing to do with the profit motive.

He did not ask what she thought of it. If he had she would have returned a guarded answer after the subtle rebuff he had inflicted on her during lunch.

But to Davina, when they had lingered on the loggia outside the master suite after the others had moved on, she admitted that she had never seen a house so perfect in every aspect and, consequently, so daunting to a designer-decorator.

'I think John must have marriage in mind. Prosper says I'm incurably romantic, and certainly John's reputation is not that of a hearth-and-home type. But even an inveterate womaniser may meet his match sooner or later. I have the feeling this house was built for someone special, not just as a holiday place,' said the artist's wife, running her fingers along the smooth, sunwarmed stone of the top of the balustrade.

'Has he been an inveterate womaniser?' Valissa could not help asking.

'Oh, yes—although not in a beastly way. I mean there are men of great wealth who have a succession of girls—lovely bodies but empty heads, mostly—as their temporary companions. Temporary being the operative word. John's relationships aren't of that order. All the women his name has been linked with have been intelligent and charming, usually women with careers. I can think of a singer, and an actress, and a cellist he met at our house who held him for more than six months. But I shouldn't be gossiping about him, and we're falling behind the rest of the tour,' she finished, looking embarrassed.

When they had seen the whole place—much of it cluttered with plasterers' and carpenters' equipment which, today being Sunday, was not in use—they returned to the launch.

As it came alongside the yacht's ladder, Dion said, 'Sit tight, will you, Valissa.'

She waited while he and the seamen ensured that, one by one, the others stepped safely from the boat to the foot of the ladder.

Then, to her, he said briskly, 'We're remaining here for the night. Costas will run you back to Loggos.' He must have heard her tell Gaia where she was staying. 'I shall be busy for some days, but I know where to find you when I want you. Meanwhile I suggest you make the most of your holiday. You'll have little time for relaxation once I put you to work.'

He stepped from the launch, and gave a signal to the seaman.

'Oh, are you leaving?' called his sister, looking down from the deck.

The motor would have drowned a reply. Valissa nodded and waved. The others, all but Dion, waved to her as the launch sped away, trailing a flurry of foam.

For three days she went for long walks in a countryside rich in spring flowers. Among the people staying at Loggos, whom she met in the tavernas at night, were several on a wild flower holiday led by a botanist from Kew Gardens.

Apparently walking parties in search of the many species of orchids on Paxos took place for two weeks every spring. Aided by a booklet on the island's flowers and their habitats, Valissa was able to identify quite a large number in the course of her own solitary walks.

But often she walked without seeing the beauty around her, her expression troubled as she remembered Dion's unfriendly dismissal, and Davina Arnold's conjecture that the house had been built for 'someone special'.

Because he had sent for her to decorate it, there were times when she could almost convince herself that she hadn't been mistaken in seeing his eyes light at the sight of her; that *she* was his love, and the house had been built for her to live in.

Yet if that were the case, why had he been so unpleasant to her the other day? And would John Roxburgh, in love, leave the woman of his choice out on a limb for six months while he spent several hundred thousand pounds building a house on the chance that she would wait for him indefinitely?

It could be that Roderick had reported her as saying she would never get over her love for Dion. But nothing explained why, if he loved and wanted her, he was leaving her to spend days and nights in mental torment.

The more she thought about it, the more she was forced to the painful conclusion that, if he had marriage in mind, it was no longer to her but to someone else; and sending for her to do the décor was partly because he believed her to be a good designer, and partly to punish her for turning him down in September.

In the evenings, after supper, she would return to the apartment and sketch all she could remember of the house and its special features. She read and re-read his brief.

No white walls. No wrought iron. No silk. Only wool, linen and cotton fabrics. Reading lights by every chair. Storage for three thousand books and five hundred records.

Function rather than effect should dictate the design of the interior. The general impression should be international; and the furnishings neither exclusively modern nor exclusively traditional, but a compound of the best of many centuries including our own—was his summing-up.

On the evening of her fifth night at Loggos, Valissa had returned to the apartment after supper, and was lying on the divan with a book propped against her updrawn

knees, but her mind on the house and its owner, when
there was a knock at the door.

It was unlikely to be Anna. There was only one other
person it could be—or a messenger from him.

Calling out, '*Mia stighmi,*' to gain a few seconds' grace,
she leapt from the bed and dashed to the drawer where
she kept her cosmetics and hairbrush. A few strokes with
the spiral brush were all there was time for.

It was Dion himself who was standing outside.

'Good evening, Valissa.'

As she stepped back, he ducked his tall head to avoid
the low lintel and strolled to the centre of the room.

'How long will it take you to pack?'

'To pack?' Was he sending her away? At this hour of
night?

'I've cancelled the booking which was made for you at
the hotel'—her heart sank, she felt physically sick—'and
it won't be convenient for you to remain here in Loggos.
We can accommodate you on *Selene*. My sister and her
family and my other guests have gone home. The landscape designer has arrived. While you and he are beginning your work, I have matters to occupy me for some
days. I shall be available to you both in the evenings if
necessary. You have no objection to living afloat for the
time being, have you?'

'No . . . none at all.' Oh, the blessed relief of not being
summarily dismissed for an offence which he hadn't yet
explained or allowed her to defend herself against!

'Right: then I'll go and explain the situation to your
maid while you get your things together. It won't take
you more than half an hour, will it?'

'Less. Fifteen minutes.'

'Good.' He walked out, closing the door after him.

Valissa flew about, flinging clothes into her suitcase,
and shoes and toilet things into a grip. It didn't matter if
they weren't well packed. She would be unpacking them
again in a short time.

When Dion reappeared she was checking to make sure
she had overlooked nothing.

'Ready?' He picked up her baggage.

Valissa took a final look around before she nodded.

At the foot of the steps Anna was waiting to say goodbye and receive the key. Impulsively Valissa bent to hug her, the Greek woman being much shorter and stockier than herself. She put a wrapped parcel into Anna's hands.

'For you . . . from England,' she said, in her uncertain Greek.

'What did you give her?' Dion asked, a few minutes later, as they were walking along the waterfront.

'Only a couple of sun-tops and a cotton skirt. Her children are always beautifully turned out, but I noticed she wore the same two dresses all the time I was staying here before. Fortunately English stores always stock summer clothes ages before the weather there starts to be summery.'

The launch was moored at the far end of the quay. There was no sign of Costas.

When Dion had stowed her luggage, and turned to help her step aboard, she paused, pointing to the building where the residue from the olives was processed.

'There's a terracotta head on top of that building which I'm sure your landscape designer would love to get his hands on for a feature for your garden.'

'Is there? I daresay it gives a good deal of pleasure where it is, if not to the locals, to some of the visitors,' Dion answered, as he handed her aboard. 'Deanery has a good selection to choose from. I've been picking up pieces for my garden for four or five years. They've been stored at the villa in Tuscany which I've had on lease for several years. At one time I intended to make it my permanent home, but Italy has become too lawless for my liking. The children of rich men are always at some risk, unfortunately, but the risk is much higher in certain countries.'

He started the motor, and they had no more conversation until, as they drew near the yacht—a spectacular sight with her white hull reflecting the moonlight and most of her portholes alight—a steward and a seaman came down the ladder, one to take charge of the luggage and the other of the launch.

'Is your landscape designer Peter Deanery?' asked Valissa, as they mounted to the deck.

'Yes. Do you know him?'

'*Of* him.' To anyone interested in gardens on the grand scale, Deanery was among the most inspired of garden designers.

'Come and meet him. I left him in the saloon,' said Dion.

'There's just one thing. . . .'

'Yes?'

She glanced about her, but there was no one within earshot.

'I—I'm not sure what to call you from now on. Mr Roxburgh . . . or John . . . or. . . .'

'Call me Dion as you've always done.'

Any encouragement she might have derived from his permission to continue the privilege—as his sister had called it—was cancelled by the anything but friendly look he bent upon her as he gave it.

In the restful if rather neutral comfort of the saloon, a thickset man with a large head and black-rimmed spectacles was immersed in an oversize book of colour plates. He glanced up as they entered, rising at the sight of Valissa. Dion introduced him to her.

'Are you an American, Miss Cornford?' Peter Deanery enquired, as they shook hands.

She guessed that he asked the question because the United States had far more professional decorators than countries in Europe, and he would not expect Dion to use an unknown designer.

'I'm English. The reason you've never heard of me is that I'm here to do the groundwork for Eliot Rutherford,' she explained.

'Oh, indeed? He and I have worked together—in the sense of designing for the same client—on a number of occasions.'

'What will you drink, Valissa?' Dion put in.

'A gin and tonic, please. Not very much gin.'

He did not ring for a steward but attended to the drinks himself, adding ice and lemon to hers, and pouring another whisky and soda for Peter Deanery. Then he asked them to excuse him for ten minutes.

By the time he came back they had sized each other up. Valissa had decided she liked the landscape designer, and he was being very affable to her.

Presently he remarked that he had set out from his home very early and would like to go to bed. When she would have followed his example, Dion said, 'I've a couple of things to give you, Valissa.'

When the other man had said goodnight and left them alone together, he gave her a full set of the architect's drawings for the house, and an inventory of all the pictures, with their sizes and descriptions of their mounts and frames, he wished to hang there.

'Which to group, and which to hang individually, I leave to your discretion,' he told her.

'This is invaluable. Thank you,' she answered, glancing through the neatly typed list which seemed to include a very wide range of art.

'Although all my crew are Greek, your stewardess, Mrs Wesley, is English. She will have unpacked for you, but I told her you wouldn't need any further attention tonight. I'll show you to your quarters, shall I?'

'Thank you, but . . . but if you're not in a hurry to go to bed, could we talk for a few minutes?'

'There are occasions when I like to go to bed early'— his glance swept appraisingly over the contours revealed by the fluid blue jersey shirt-dress she had put on for dinner—'but unfortunately I don't think this is one of them.'

Valissa felt her colour rising. It wasn't the first time he had looked at her desirously, but somehow before it had been different. Now there was no element of tenderness in his expression. His grey eyes were narrowed and predatory.

'What was it you wanted to talk about?' he prompted.

'The other day . . . after your nephew had hurt himself . . . I asked why you had pretended to be someone other than John Roxburgh, and why you intended to continue the deception this time. You were going to explain, but just then Prosper Arnold came up to us.'

'I'll tell you; but first I'd like a truthful reply to one question. Think about it for a moment before you answer.' He paused. 'If, when I asked you to marry me, you had known I was John Roxburgh, would you have broken our brief engagement?'

Valissa didn't need to think. 'No, because then it would have been a different situation.'

'Exactly.' His tone was caustic. 'But I would have been the same man; and although you may think it eccentric, I prefer to have a wife who cares for me, regardless of my material assets.'

His sarcasm was like the flick of a lash.

'I don't give a hoot for your assets,' she retorted hotly. 'At least not on this lavish scale. But if I had known that you had at least *some* means behind you, of course it would have made a difference. I—I loved you very much, Dion. It made me very unhappy to have to break off our engagement.'

'You use the past tense, I notice. You've recovered, apparently.'

She looked down at the list in her hand, unable to meet his hard stare as she said, 'People don't recover from loving. If it really is love, it's incurable.'

'Most affecting, Valissa,' he said dryly. 'But not entirely convincing. I wonder why you didn't mention your undying devotion in the letter you wrote to me recently? No doubt because it had occurred to you that John Roxburgh would have a great deal more to offer than Dion Stefanides.'

'How dare you! Such a thing never even occurred to me, and you have no right to suggest it,' she flared indignantly.

He gave a harsh laugh. 'Then I'll make a different suggestion. You tell me you're still in love with me, and I—although no longer in a marrying mood—still find you extremely desirable. As we live in an era when many people live together informally, why don't we do that? As my close friend you'll have everything that my wife would have, except a legal contract, and is that really so important?'

Something seemed to shrivel inside her. This was not the same man who, on that lovely day at Parga, had said to her—I want you. Not just for a few nights of pleasure, for the rest of my life. To be the mother of my sons.

'It isn't the contract which matters. It's the commitment,' she said sadly. 'The belief that love can last a life-time. I'm afraid I don't want to be your girl-friend. It's not a rôle which appeals to me—although as such things go, I'm sure it must rank very high. May I go to my cabin now, please?'

'If you insist. You would sleep more soundly if you came and shared mine,' he said mockingly. 'Don't look so put out. Have you forgotten the night before you went back to England, when you actually begged me to make love to you? It was you who shied from a commitment on that occasion.'

'That was then. This is now,' she said stiffly.

Someone knocked at the door. A moment later a steward came in with a paper on a silver salver. As he presented it, he spoke to his employer in Greek.

Dion replied in the same language. Then, in English, he added, 'Elefterios will show you to your quarters. Goodnight, Valissa.'

She was already awake when, at seven o'clock, her stewardess brought her a goblet of fresh orange juice.

'Good morning, madam. Mr Roxburgh thought you might prefer fruit juice to early morning tea,' she said, setting the tray on the night table. 'I don't know whether this is the time you like to be called. Perhaps you'd prefer a little earlier?'

'This is fine, Mrs Wesley, thank you . . . and thank you for unpacking for me last night. I'm afraid my case was in rather a shambles. I wasn't expecting to leave my apart-ment in Loggos, and I tossed my clothes in all anyhow so as not to keep Mr Roxburgh waiting.'

'I guessed that you'd left in a hurry. Shall I run you a bath, or do you like a shower in the morning?'

'A bath would be lovely. Then, if I can muster the courage to have a swim at midday, I'll shampoo and shower before dinner.'

'The water won't be warm in April, although Master John swims all year round. Oh, hark at me—Master John indeed! It's a long time since he's been that. My aunt was housekeeper to his mother, so from when I was a girl in my teens I was used to hearing him called Master

John,' explained Mrs Wesley. 'Has he shown you the portrait of his mother which hangs in his study, madam?'

Valissa shook her head.

'She was beautiful,' said the stewardess. 'The most beautiful woman, my aunt said, she'd ever laid eyes on. She was a film actress, you know, before Mr Roxburgh's father married her, and she gave it all up for love of him. It was a terrible tragedy when she died so young. Dear me, I musn't stand talking. I'll go and run your bath.'

Valissa had breakfast with Peter Deanery, after which they both went ashore.

Wandering through the house for the second time, lingering in rooms where the workmen were no longer busy, Valissa agreed with Dion's dictum against white walls. In a small, simple dwelling, sparsely furnished, the starkness of white could be appropriate. But this house demanded colour; all the colours which were her own favourites—chartreuse, terracotta and lemon, dull olive green and pale blue, soft rose and warm, glowing apricot.

At noon, after working for three hours, she went down to the bay to find out for herself if the sea was impossibly cold. It looked as clear and inviting as it had in September.

It seemed freezing at first, but after about twenty strokes she found it becoming less icy. She was a hundred yards out, relaxing after a vigorous crawl, when she saw the launch coming towards her.

'You must be tougher than you look,' called Dion, when Costas had cut the engine and brought the boat gliding almost to a standstill close by her. There was also a steward on board.

Forgetting for a moment how things stood between them, Valissa called back, 'It's only getting in which is painful. After that it's invigorating.'

'I know. I'm about to join you.' He was shedding his shirt and pants.

A few moments later he dived from the launch and disappeared.

'We're bringing you a picnic lunch,' he said when he surfaced beside her. 'I didn't expect to find you swimming. How did you sleep?'—white teeth flashing.

'Excellently, thank you.' Valissa struck out for the shore.

She had no hope of beating him to it; she knew that before she started. But when she stood up in the shallows, not far from where he was waiting, she wasn't prepared for him to come swiftly towards her and take her in his arms.

The other men were on the way up to the house, Costas with a hamper balanced on his head, and the steward carrying a cold box. But if they should pause and look down they would see her and their employer, and she wouldn't have expected Dion to kiss her in public.

Nor was it a playful embrace, or a quick teasing kiss which he planted on her startled mouth.

They might have been Adam and Eve, or two happy castaways free to make love where they pleased, the way he strained her against him, and forced a long, passionate kiss on her.

She was trembling when at last he raised his head. 'A foretaste of the pleasures in store for us,' he told her, with the mocking smile she hated. 'You might as well surrender gracefully. You will surrender—it's inevitable.'

Dazed by the fierce, searching kiss, she watched him pick up a robe which the steward had left beside her towel. Instead of putting it on, he wrapped it round her shaking form, pulled her towel round his neck, and picked her up.

'Dion ... please ... put me down,' she protested.

'You didn't object the last time I did this, my lovely. You were very submissive. Remember? *I* remember it clearly.'

At the top of the staircase, Peter was waiting for them. 'By George, you've got more guts than I have! The sea is only fit for seals at this time of year. I felt it on the way across.'

'And Valissa has no protective blubber,' said Dion, with a glance which, in spite of the robe still around her, made her feel naked.

'Nor have you, for that matter,' said Peter. 'You must be in tip-top condition. Even if I were ten years younger, I couldn't pound up those stairs with a slim but tall girl in my arms.'

'She'd stayed in too long and was shivering,' said Dion, knowing full well that her tremors had nothing to do with her bathe. He pulled up the hood of the beach robe to cover her wet hair. 'Sit down and I'll dry your feet for you.'

The steward had set out three deck chairs and, nearby, was laying a table.

'What about you?' Valissa objected, as he pushed her into a chair.

'I wasn't in the water as long as you were, and anyway I'm used to it.'

She watched him towelling her feet, his broad back and shoulders still beaded with bright drops of water. He had not lost his tan as she had. Probably he was never away from the sun for more than a week at a time.

Pan ... Apollo ... Helios, the sun god. With his thick curls and strong-boned Greek profile, Dion could have modelled for any one of them. How could she resist him if he wanted her? Did she want to? For whom was she saving herself, if not for this man she loved who no longer loved her?

CHAPTER EIGHT

For dinner that night Valissa wore a dress she had bought on her last day in London for the delectation of Dion Stefanides.

Although ready-to-wear, inexpensive, and not to be compared with the designer clothes worn by the women of John Roxburgh's world, nevertheless it did something for her. It was reddish-brown silk, a colour close to her hair, and it made her eyes look their bluest. The style was simple, with a deep V neckline and close-fitting bodice fastened with silk-covered buttons, as were the cuffs of the sleeves. The skirt was straight, slightly gathered at the front between the seams containing the slit pockets. It was one of those timeless classics which look nothing on a hanger. On Valissa's slender figure it was unexpectedly alluring, showing the shape of her breasts, a good deal of them being revealed in full by the depth of the V which had made it necessary to buy a special cutaway bra to go under the dress.

She had also bought brown kid sandals made of a minimum of straps, and a tiny bag on a shoulder-cord with a tassel.

When she entered the saloon, Dion and Peter were chatting. They both rose and bade her good evening, and Dion walked towards her. Peter moved to replace a book he had taken from a bank of shelves and to pause there, studying the other titles.

'Gin and tonic for you?' Dion asked, taking note of her dress.

'Yes, please.'

'But not too much gin,' he said, remembering her qualification of the night before.

The saloon was the full width of *Selene*'s nine-metre beam, which meant that someone on one side wouldn't necessarily hear a remark made by someone on the other, especially if there was music playing and the speaker dropped his voice slightly, as Dion did when he added, 'I see we are now in agreement on the subject of inevitability. You wouldn't have worn that dress if it were otherwise.'

She moved with him to the drinks cupboard concealed in the hardwood panelling which covered all the bulkheads.

'I'm in a difficult position,' she answered, in a low tone. 'I'm here to work. Eliot won't be pleased if I leave before completing my assignment. I don't want to jeopardise my job.'

'If that's supposed to make me feel a rat, it doesn't succeed,' he said, dropping ice into a tall glass. 'I don't think Eliot would sack you if you fled back to London, and told him that Roxburgh was an unprincipled satyr who wanted you to sleep with him. But if it makes it easier for you to feel that I'm putting the pressure on, I have no objection.'

'Aren't you putting the pressure on? You know casual liaisons aren't my style.'

'My dear Valissa, never say I didn't do my best to make an honest woman of you! You wouldn't have it.' He gave her the drink he had made for her. 'Whoever designed that believed in the definition that a successful dress is one men want to take off—as I shall perhaps, later.'

He turned and walked back towards the other man. 'Another drink for you, Peter?'

'No, thanks. There's a limit to the amount of alcohol I can take when I'm working. Too much whisky and too many late nights aren't conducive to early rising once one's on the wrong side of forty.'

'I never mix grape and grain as you two do,' remarked Dion. 'You should change to *ouzo*. It goes better with wine.'

'What is it made from?' asked Peter.

'Sweet grapes, raisins and about twenty herbs including, of course, the anise which gives it its flavour.'

'I've heard too much *ouzo* can give one a blistering hangover.'

'So they say. I've never experienced it myself, but yoghurt is the prescribed antidote.'

Presently they had dinner, a delicious meal including, as a savoury, marrowbones.

Valissa had noticed the thin, elongated silver spoon which was part of her place setting, and had recognised what it was. But she had never actually eaten the dish before and was interested to see how it was presented.

The bones, each one wrapped in a napkin, were brought to the table standing upright in a silver dish. They were served with pieces of hot, dry toast on to which the marrow was scooped out and then dusted with pepper.

After dinner they returned to the saloon where Dion suggested they should conclude the evening with some music.

'Where do your musical preferences lie, Valissa?' he asked her.

'I like Rachmaninov's piano concertos,' she answered, choosing at random from a catholic taste which embraced music as wide in range as his collection of paintings.

They listened to two of the four concertos after which, when her favourite, the Third, had come to an end, Peter rose and wished them goodnight.

'More music, or bed for you, too?' Dion asked, deliberately baiting her.

All the time the music had been playing, she had been aware of his scrutiny. He had chosen to sit in a position from which, without Peter noticing, he could feast his eyes on her silk-clad body and slender legs.

Once or twice she had glanced at him, only to look swiftly away from the half-smiling sensual mouth, and the gleaming grey eyes.

Before she could reply, the telephone started to chirp.

'Excuse me.' He swung out of his chair to answer it. 'Roxburgh.' After listening for some seconds, he said, 'I'll take it in my study.' To Valissa, he added explanatorily, 'A call from my New York office.'

She rose. 'Then I'll say goodnight.'

They walked to the door, Dion moving ahead, as she thought to open it for her. Instead he held it closed, reaching out his other arm to draw her to him. But the kiss she expected did not happen. He held her for a few moments, his arm behind her, his hand moving possessively on her waist and hip as he looked at the tender flesh exposed by the deep décolletage.

'I hope this won't take too long. Unfortunately people are still working on the other side of the Atlantic, and business must come before pleasure.'

His arm slackened. As she drew back, he bent and kissed her, just above the topmost button of her dress. Then he opened the door and stood aside to let her pass.

In her luxurious blue and white stateroom, Valissa switched on the light and crossed to the dressing-table. She sank on to the padded bench and stared wide-eyed at her reflection, her breathing fast and unsteady after her recent experience.

She could still feel the warmth of his lips between her breasts, and the pressure of his square, forceful chin made darker at this hour of night by the shadow of the stubble which, with its slight roughness, had emphasised the intimacy of the caress.

It took her several minutes to pull herself together; and even then she was not fully in control. How could she be when she had no idea how long it would be before he came to her?

With fingers made clumsy by nervousness, she unbuttoned her cuffs and reached for the tag of the zipper at the nape of her neck. As well as the spotted net bra, she was wearing black satin French knickers and Dior tights. She took everything off and put on her nightdress. It had been spread across the turned-down bed. She had only this one nightie with her, and during the day it had been washed and ironed. Where the lace had been coming unstitched it had been neatly repaired.

By the time she had put away her clothes, removed her make-up and brushed her teeth, about fifteen minutes had passed since she and Dion had separated outside the saloon.

Wondering how other girls behaved in these circumstances—but who else would be as unversed as she was at her age?—she climbed into bed. It was a single bed, but considerably wider than her bed in London. She sat up, hugging her knees, her eyes on the door, her inside a tight knot of tension as she waited for it to open.

'A note from Mr Roxburgh, madam,' said Mrs Wesley, when Valissa was fully awake.

She had been roused by a gentle tinkling sound which turned out to have been the stewardess tapping the glass containing her early morning fruit juice with the pencil from the telephone pad.

'Thank you.' Valissa opened the sealed envelope and withdrew the sheet of paper inside it.

I'm sorry about last night, Dion had written. *A critical situation had arisen which occupied me for over an hour. By the time I was free you were in a deep sleep. We must hope for better luck tonight.*

Mrs Wesley had already departed, and therefore was not a witness to the vivid flush which stained Valissa's face and throat as she realised that Dion must have stood by her bed, debating whether to waken her and finally deciding against it. It must have been he who had turned out the lights and drawn back the curtains from the two portholes.

In a way she wished he had woken her. If he had, she would not have another day of tension ahead of her. The suspense would be over, the die cast. She would at last have experienced love's 'right true end', instead of being uneasily aware that, even now, he could not force her to remain aboard *Selene* if she insisted upon leaving.

As he had said to her last night, there was no outside pressure to make her enter a relationship which was not her style. The only pressure was her love for him; her feeling that, if she did not accept the casual affair which was all there could be between them now, she would go to her grave without ever knowing complete fulfilment.

She might not actually die a virgin; but even if, eventually, she married someone else and achieved a modest degree of happiness, she would always be haunted by the longing to have slept and woken in Dion's arms.

He did not repeat his lunchtime visit to the house.

Again, a delicious cold collation was brought over and served in a sheltered place outside, but she and Peter ate *à deux*, discussing their ideas for the house and its grounds, and finding themselves more and more in accord.

He did not refer to his private life, nor did he enquire about hers. Their conversation never strayed from their professional interests, and this was a welcome distraction from the thoughts which had kept interfering with her concentration during the morning.

The launch came to fetch them at three, which was earlier than the previous day, but they concluded there must be some reason for their time on the island being cut short.

'Anyway, I must get a report off to Eliot. He'll expect to be kept fully informed,' said Valissa, on the way back to the yacht.

Before settling down to type a letter to Eliot on her portable typewriter, she thought she would have a shower, protecting her hair with the bath cap which was only one of the things provided for the use of the stateroom's occupant.

Nothing that a man or woman could conceivably want, but might have neglected to bring with them, was not to be found there. A cupboard in the bathroom, and another in the bedroom, carried stocks of everything from several kinds of toothpaste and brushes to extra hangers for the closets and pillows with synthetic and herbal fillings for guests who were allergic to feathers or found that hops helped them to sleep better.

When, naked, her skin sleek with talc, Valissa opened the bathroom door and returned to the bedroom, she was startled to find it in twilight. The lined curtains, open ten minutes ago, were now closed, and only a fraction of the brilliant sunlight outside was able to penetrate the stateroom.

Her exclamation of surprise was rapidly followed by an even more startled cry when, padding across the thick pale blue carpet to open them, she was seized from behind by strong hands and spun into a crushing embrace.

She had just time to gasp his name before Dion's mouth closed on hers.

Later—how much later she couldn't tell, having lost all sense of time and even, for a while, of place—he moved his head. Speaking close to her ear, he said, 'You little fool. In God's name, why didn't you tell me?'

She found it difficult to bestir herself from the strange trancelike state which had followed the frenzy before.

'Would it have made any difference?' she asked softly.

Then she wished she had answered differently, because his reaction to her question was to roll away and sit up.

'*Khristos!* What do you take me for? A man with no scruples at all? I have some principles left. I don't cuckold faithful husbands, and I don't seduce virgins,' he answered, with angry impatience.

'I'm not seventeen . . . or even eighteen or nineteen. You gave me plenty of chance to avoid what just happened. I chose not to.' She stretched out her hand to stroke his back.

Her touch made him turn, putting one hand on the bed on the far side of her to support him as he leaned above her. There was just enough light for her to see that he was frowning.

'It must have hurt damnably.'

'A little, but'—quoting one of her favourite books—'it was a "lovely cruelty" which everyone has to go through.' Valissa put up her arms, wanting to pull him down to her. 'I'm glad it happened with you.'

Again it was the wrong thing to say. Dion removed her hands from his shoulders and turned away, rising this time and going to uncurtain the ports.

The afternoon light flooded in, and the deckhead gleamed with reflections of the sunlight on the calm sea. Dion glanced at her, stretched on the bed, then he disappeared into the bathroom. Seconds later she heard the shower running.

Reluctantly she sat up, still feeling languorous after the wild storm of feeling he had induced in her. She had been prepared for the first time to be far from ecstatic; but it had been better than she had expected. Wonderful, until the very end. She had no doubt that, if he had known it was the first time for her, he would have hurt her even less. But it seemed that if he had known that, he wouldn't have taken her at all.

Perhaps he was disappointed; having hoped to find in her a partner as skilled as himself.

When he came back she was wrapped in her robe and brushing her hair at the dressing-table.

Dion, a towel round his hips, was rubbing his hair with another.

'We'll be married as soon as it can be arranged. Probably next week,' he told her briskly.

She stopped brushing and stared at him. 'Married? B-but the night before last you said you were not in a marrying mood any more!'

'I no longer have a choice.'

'That's ridiculous, Dion,' she said abruptly. 'You don't have to marry me merely because I was a virgin. I——I don't want to be married on that basis.'

'You also have no choice,' he informed her. 'If you think there will be no outcome because it was the first time, you're making a mistake which a great many girls have regretted a few weeks later. And if you imagine, in that eventuality, I'll allow you to avoid the consequences of this afternoon, you're equally mistaken. That recourse can leave psychological scars which aren't necessary in this case.'

' "This case" may never happen. Wouldn't it be better to wait and see before plunging into a marriage you don't really want?'

He tossed aside the hand towel and folded his arms across his chest, looking down at her with a cynical expression.

'It's time I married and had children. I daresay we shall get on as well as most couples. In the meantime, if our relationship is to be a permanent one, I prefer that my staff shouldn't regard you in any other light. I shan't come here again.'

He began to put on the clothes he had already discarded when she entered and found the room in half-darkness.

'What if I refuse to marry you?' she asked, as he dressed.

'You won't. The night before last you professed to be incurably in love with me,' he said dryly. 'Even if you weren't, it would be foolish to turn down all I have to offer, don't you think?' He came to where she was sitting and put his hand under her chin. 'And the next time we go to bed together, you'll enjoy it much more than today. You may have been a virgin, but no one could accuse you of being a prude.'

He drew her to her feet and tilted her head back to kiss her, his hand slipping slowly down her throat to slide inside the front of her robe and close on one small tingling breast.

'Please, Dion . . . tell me you love me,' she breathed, when he freed her lips.

His hand went on gently caressing her. But there was no warmth in his eyes as he met the appeal in hers. She had a humiliating feeling that although it was too soon for his desire to have revived, it amused him to stir her senses and make her long to repeat the pleasures of half an hour ago.

'Don't expect life to give you everything. It never does. That's something I should have remembered,' he said, on a note of irony. 'I must go now. I'll see you at dinner.'

When she entered the saloon, later, still racked by uncertainty, although now for a different reason, Dion said to her and to Peter, 'Tonight we'll drink only champagne.' To the older man, he added, 'Valissa and I are going to be married.' He turned to her. 'Until we have a chance to choose an engagement ring, I'd like you to wear a ring I happen to have on board.'

But it wasn't the gold ram's head ring which was in the box which he took from his pocket. It was a much more valuable spiral of platinum encrusted with diamonds and sapphires.

'This was one of my mother's rings,' he explained, taking her hand and slipping the ring on her finger.

By which time it was too late to protest that she hadn't yet made up her mind. Short of causing an embarrassing scene, there was nothing to be done but to accept Peter's congratulations and good wishes.

'Thank you. I'd be grateful if you'd keep the news to yourself for the time being,' said Dion. 'I detest personal publicity, and shan't make a public announcement until we return from our honeymoon.'

They were married in one of the smallest of the island's eighty-three churches and chapels. At his mother's wish, Dion had been baptised in the Orthodox faith, and it was the simplest way to avoid attracting the attention of press and television reporters.

The church was decorated with spring flowers, including most of the ten species of wild orchid to be found on Paxos, and lilies, starry white alliums, sprays of broom and many sweet-scented herbs.

Valissa wore a simple dress of ivory chiffon, chosen from several brought on approval from Athens by Dion's youngest aunt who was married to an Athenian and whose two children stood on either side of the bridal couple holding tall, thick candles made of beeswax.

In front of them was a table covered with a white cloth. On this stood a glass of wine and two wedding rings.

Although the church itself was very plain with lime-washed walls and deal stalls, the bearded archimandrite who took the service wore colourful vestments of white and gold brocade embroidered in scarlet and green.

Parts of the service he translated into English so that the bride, and the other English people present—Peter, *Selene*'s captain and Mrs Wesley—could follow them.

The rings—the smaller with *Dionysios* engraved inside it, and the larger with *Valissa*—were blessed and exchanged. The bride and groom sipped the wine which symbolised the joy and bitterness they would share in the years ahead.

Coronets made of leather and lemon blossom were held above their heads by their sponsor, Dion's aunt, and then exchanged, and exchanged again. They were taken three times round the altar in the ritual 'Dance of Isaiah', the priest intoning as he led them.

Soon the ceremony was over, and they were a married couple—'those whom God has united and no man should attempt to part.'

When Dion had suggested postponing a honeymoon cruise until the house was closer to being habitable, Valissa had not objected. In any case the luxury of life on the yacht, and the beauty of her present anchorage, far surpassed the settings of most people's honeymoons.

So their wedding evening was spent in the owner's suite where they dined alone with the yacht lying outside Gaios harbour so that Dion's aunt and uncle could be hosts at a party ashore for Peter and all but a handful of *Selene*'s crew.

'You're not wearing your ring,' she said, noticing this during dinner.

'No, I've taken it off. The exchange of rings was an integral part of the service, and most married men on the Continent do wear a ring. But it goes against my English grain,' he answered. 'My father left me his signet ring, but I don't wear that either. You aren't superstitious about rings, are you? I know some women feel it's bad luck to take off their wedding rings.'

'No, I'm not superstitious,' she said lightly.

But she couldn't help feeling hurt that he had removed it so soon. His ring had been gold, hers platinum to match the ring of his mother's which she had asked to keep rather than choosing a new one. She would have preferred the ram's head, but perhaps he no longer possessed it, and anyway it was part of a time which could never be recaptured unless she could somehow reanimate the love Dion had felt for her then.

Secretly she was determined that unless that day came, she would never ask him for anything or express any interest in jewels, furs or any other costly things. Perhaps, gradually, he would be convinced that his wealth was not important to her; that she had come back to Paxos hoping to marry Dion Stefanides.

Her decision was tested after dinner when the steward had cleared the table and said goodnight and, short of a fire breaking out or some similar emergency, they would be undisturbed until the following morning.

'I haven't yet shown you your wedding present,' said Dion, swinging aside a mirror, the frame of which was hinged to the bulkhead to disguise the presence of a safe.

'By the way, this operates on a combination known only to me and Captain Greene and, in future, to you.' He told her what it was.

From the safe he took a flat round leather case which he put on the table beneath the safe before pushing the mirror back in place. Beckoning her to him, he said, 'This won't show to advantage over your shirt. You'd better take it off.'

Earlier she had changed her wedding dress for a silk shirt and long crêpe skirt with a slit up the side.

When she hesitated to do as he told her, he said, 'I am your husband now, and it's only your shirt you need remove—for the moment.'

Her shyness not eased by the mocking addition, Valissa slipped it off. Half an hour's sunbathe each day had restored the becoming pale amber tint to her skin. The underthings she was wearing were part of a set of trousseau lingerie given to her by Dion's aunt who, like her dead sister, had become a much more sophisticated person than their countrified mother who had never ventured beyond Paxos.

She saw Dion's gaze linger appreciatively on the wisp of primrose crêpe-de-chine and écru lace which had a matching pair of micro briefs, and a suspender belt to fasten the stockings which had seemed more feminine and glamorous than tights on her wedding day—even if it was not the wedding day she had hoped for.

'Turn your back to the mirror until I've put it on,' he said.

She felt the coldness of metal on her skin and, without looking down, was aware of something sparkling and flashing.

'There: now you may look.' He took her by the shoulders and turned her to face the looking glass.

The collar of diamonds made her catch her breath. In a setting as delicate as snow crystals, they winked and glittered in the light from the wall-lamps which flanked the mirror.

'Do you like it?' he asked. Without waiting for her answer, he pressed his lips to her smooth golden shoulder, his fingertips tracing light patterns on her upper arms.

Excitement quickened in the pit of her stomach. She saw, and he saw as well, the breathless parting of her lips, the sudden budding of her breasts beneath the thin primrose silk.

His mouth moved to the nape of her neck and his fingers to the clip of the bra. She gave a small choking cry as, at the same instant, she felt the soft bite on her neck and his warm palms replaced the fabric.

'Have you been impatient, Valissa?' he murmured huskily, as long shudders coursed through her body.

'Yes ... yes ... oh, *yes*!' she whispered, all the earlier shyness forgotten as his lips and his hands worked their magic on her.

The mirror reflected his conquest. Through half-closed eyes she saw herself leaning against him, her head arched against his shoulder as he nibbled the lobe of her ear, her instinctively sinuous movements—like a cat which wants to be stroked—making the diamonds a blaze of white fire.

'Please ... take off the necklace ... it may be damaged,' she murmured.

'It won't be. I like it on you. You should always wear diamonds—and nothing else.' He was undoing the zip of her skirt, pushing it down over her hips until it slithered to her feet. 'How does this pretty nonsense undo?'—investigating the suspender belt.

She let him find out for himself, her own fingers searching frantically for the clasp of the necklace, an almost impossible task when his very touch was a caress. Long before her fumbling fingers had mastered the intricate catch, he had found the fastenings he wanted. Her shoes, stockings and the suspender belt had all been removed and discarded, leaving only the minimal briefs.

As, kneeling on one leg behind her, he stroked her thighs and kissed her hips, she felt the clasp come apart. With a gasp of relief she restored the diamonds to their case, too distracted to be capable of fitting them into the channel in the black velvet, but at least safely, thankfully rid of them.

Dion turned her to face him, his hands spreading over her buttocks, his dark, curly head at her waist as he kissed a path down from her navel. Suddenly she found herself being pulled forward over his shoulder as he rose to his feet and carried her through to his bedroom where, while they were dining, the wide bed had been turned down on both sides and her trousseau nightgown, of white chiffon and lace insertion threaded with primrose satin ribbons, laid out for her.

Not ungently, Dion tumbled her, flushed from the brief fireman's lift, on to the centre of the bed. Only one lamp was alight, its subdued glow making the severely masculine stateroom seem cosier than it had earlier, when she had changed her wedding dress there.

Valissa lay where he had tossed her, not afraid and yet not relaxed. She was still almost a virgin, and she knew it was not the, to him, trifling exertion of carrying her which was making his chest rise and fall as he loomed, tall and powerful, above her; breathing hard, but still in sufficient command of himself to deal with the buckle of his belt and the buttons of his shirt much more swiftly than she had released the clasp on the necklace.

Watching him rapidly shedding his clothes, she remembered how, after the first time, he had promised that the next time they made love she would enjoy it much more; and, while they were in the other room, his caresses had given her pleasure.

But now, all at once, he looked strangely fierce and impatient; not the laughing-eyed Greek she had loved at the end of last summer, but a hard, ruthless man of the world who had had many women before her, and perhaps would have many more, once her body had lost its novelty for him.

Unclothed himself, he leaned down and deftly removed her one remaining scanty covering. Then, starting at the curve of her instep, he began to kiss her again.

In the night, she woke up feeling thirsty. Dion seemed to be heavily asleep. Taking care not to disturb him, she slid from the bed and padded silently through his dressing-room to the bathroom, not switching on any lights until she had closed the inner door.

Eliot, who abominated as vulgar all bathrooms decor-

ated with marble or gold-plated taps in the form of dolphins or swans, would approve of John Roxburgh's bathroom. The taps were of chrome, strictly functional, and
the walls were hung with dark brown linen, most of it
covered by framed original drawings by famous cartoon-
ists of many nationalities and many periods from the
eighteenth century to the present.

Valissa drank some water and stared at herself in the
mirror behind the handbasin. Now, at last, she was fully
a woman; and it was not disappointment with her second,
more complete experience of love which made tears fill
her eyes as she put the glass back on the counter and
snatched at a towel to muffle her sobs.

Before she had fallen asleep, she had known more
ecstasy in an hour than, she suspected, most women felt
in a lifetime. Although how did anyone know the secrets
of other people's bedrooms? Who would guess that, at
five o'clock in the morning, a millionaire's bride, the
new Mrs John Roxburgh, was locked in a bathroom,
crying?

Not because her bridegroom's embraces had been dis-
tasteful or unsatisfying; but because not once had he
answered her whispered words of love with the simple
response which she longed for.

Presently she laved her face with cold water, and held
a wet, folded face-cloth against her eyes for some minutes.
Then she went quietly back to bed.

Dion himself had told her, *Don't expect life to give you
everything. It never does.*

As she lay down, it was in her mind that probably
there were many women, whose husbands were fond but
unexciting, who would willingly change places with her
for the sake of Dion's skill as a lover.

There was a movement behind her, and a strong, sure
hand on her hip turned her over on to her back. In the
dim radiance of the pre-dawn moonlight, she saw him
raise himself on one elbow.

Having lost his love, perhaps she could at least learn to
keep his desire alight for longer than anyone else had.
Reaching up to encircle his neck, she drew his head down
to hers.

Within a few days of the wedding, the helicopter pad was completed and one of the first people to take off from it was Peter Deanery, leaving to fly from Corfu to Florence, to supervise the removal of selected garden ornaments from the Tuscan villa to Paxos.

A few days later the helicopter brought in a newcomer to the island, but as he was conducted without delay from the pad to the landing stage, and thence to the yacht, Valissa did not see him until later.

She had discovered, greatly to her delight, that now it was the season of fireflies. As the light faded, they appeared; whirling about the darkening grounds like flurries of sparks from a bonfire, except that they were green instead of red.

For this reason, and because, after lunch on board, Dion would often suggest a siesta—though with no intention of sleeping—she tended to linger at the house as late as possible, using a small boat to go backwards and forwards on her own instead of depending on the launch.

'There's a guest for dinner this evening, madam. Mr Roxburgh has already changed, but he said there was no need for you to hurry your bath,' Mr Wesley told her when Valissa returned to the yacht that evening, until then unaware that she and her husband would not be dining alone in their private quarters as they had since Peter's departure.

'Who is it?' she asked the stewardess.

'Someone from England, but I believe Mr Roxburgh wants to surprise you, madam,' was all Mrs Wesley would tell her.

Could their visitor be Roderick? Valissa wondered, as she lay in her bath.

However, it was not the friend of Dion's schooldays— as she now knew Roderick to have been—but Eliot Rutherford who rose from a sofa in the saloon when she arrived there.

'Eliot! What are you doing here?' she exclaimed.

'Good evening, Valissa. Mr Roxburgh invited me here as a matter of some urgency, and I've managed to re-arrange my schedule to fit in a very brief visit,' her employer—as she still thought of him—replied, in a somewhat repressive tone.

He sounded, she thought, like a parent summoned to appear before the principal of a school because of his offspring's misdemeanours.

'Mr Roxburgh suggested that we should postpone discussing the problem which has arisen until you joined us,' he added. 'I'm sorry to hear that matters have not been progressing as smoothly as I'd hoped,' he added, frowning at her.

'That is not how I put it, Rutherford.'

Turning to look at Dion, Valissa found him regarding her with a very odd expression on his face.

'What is it? What's the matter?' she asked uneasily.

'Nothing. That is merely Rutherford's assumption,' was his calm reply. 'A few moments ago, Valissa, he was asking me if I'd met this penniless Paxiot with whom, apparently, before you left London, you were determined to live in romantic penury, to the extent of announcing that the design of my house would be your last assignment as a member of Rutherford's staff.'

Before she could react to this, Eliot said, 'But I must say I didn't think you would allow this very foolish love affair to impair your efficiency while you *are* still employed by me, Valissa. I take it that that's the basis of your dissatisfaction?' addressing this question to the other man.

'Have I mentioned my dissatisfaction?'

'No—not in so many words. But——'

'But you're mistaken,' said Dion. 'As I realise I've been mistaken. Would you excuse us for a few minutes? I have something extremely urgent to say to Valissa in private. Meanwhile, let me assure you that I didn't ask you here to complain of her. On the contrary!'

Taking her firmly by the arm, he propelled her from the saloon and past the dining-room to his study.

'Why didn't you tell me you'd given him your notice?— and the reason why you couldn't leave England until recently?' he demanded, as he closed the door.

Without waiting for her reply, he pulled her roughly into his arms, saying huskily, 'Oh, God, my poor little love! What a pigheaded brute I've been to you, refusing to believe you meant it when you told me you loved me!'

Valissa clung to him, hardly daring to believe that because of Eliot's misapprehension, the truth of her feelings for Dion had at last become clear to him.

'If I had told you, I don't think you would have been convinced,' she murmured.

'No, possibly not—not unless it was irrefutable, as it was when Rutherford announced that, the last time he saw you, you'd been hellbent on giving up everything for some sweet-talking Paxiot beach-boy,' he said, with a half-suppressed laugh.

She lifted her eyes to his and saw, with joy in her heart, the beloved dark face beginning to break into the smile he had given her often last year, but rarely since her return.

Much later that night, after Eliot had had it explained that he had been flown out from England in his client's private plane because there was now a Mrs Roxburgh whose views on interior design would carry more weight than his or those of her husband, Valissa undressed for bed in a state of unalloyed happiness.

She had left the two men still talking. But she knew from the look he had given her after she had said goodnight to Eliot that it would not be long before Dion followed her.

Meanwhile she sat brushing her hair and tapping her feet to the slow lilt of a *syrtaki* tune like the one to which he had danced with such virile grace the night they had dined at Mongonisi.

Before the tempo had begun to accelerate, he came in and paused by the door for a moment, listening, and watching her through the looking glass until she swung round to smile at him.

His muscular body beginning to move to the rhythm, he stripped off the grey linen overshirt he had worn for dinner that evening. The laughter lines down his hard cheeks deepened as he began to dance in the space between the foot of the bed and where she sat. Suddenly he was no longer the urbane financier who, a little while earlier, had been discussing world affairs with Eliot; he was simply a lithe-bodied Greek unselfconsciously expressing his feelings to music, and beckoning his bride to join him.

Later, long after he had turned off the radio and she was lying with her head on his shoulder, she said, 'One thing I don't quite understand is what, at the very beginning, you were doing at the cottage by yourself. Where was *Selene* at that time?'

'I'd lent her to someone whose wife had been seriously ill, and who needed sea air and peace. Every year, while my grandmother was alive, I used to lend the yacht to friends while I spent two weeks in Paxos, reminding myself of my origins and of the realities of life as it's lived by the majority of people. My grandmother was an extremely obstinate old woman. When she was widowed she refused to live with my aunt in Athens, and she would never let me improve the cottage for her, although I did persuade her to have the place wired.'

He paused. 'As I think I told you, she died last summer. I came back briefly for her funeral, and then for a longer period while the Connaughts were cruising off Corsica. I needed my annual "retreat", and to mull over building a place here. Not having a wife—or the prospect of one—when I arrived, it wasn't a matter of urgency. Then you came into my life—but went out of it again shortly afterwards.'

Valissa changed her position, turning over to lie facing him, her chin on the heel of one hand, her other arm on his chest.

'When *did* you decide to build the house?'

'Immediately after running into Roderick in the south of France. He told me only a fool would expect any girl of your sort to accept love in a cottage in Paxos, winter and summer. So I thought up a scheme to bring you back to the island this spring, and still keep my alter ego, Dionysios Stefanides, in existence until things were settled between us. If you were prepared to accept a future as Roxburgh's housekeeper, which I felt you might be, I would have revealed myself.'

'You never had any fears that I might have got over you, or met someone else?'

'Not really. You didn't seem the type to fall in and out of love as quickly as that. In December Roderick wrote that he'd run into you in London, looking like a shadow and obviously pining. You had actually admitted that you were, he said.'

'But you didn't feel compelled to come and comfort me?'

Dion stroked her smooth cheek with his knuckles. 'Yes—but my family responsibilities were intervening at that point. One of my Greek uncles, who has lived in the States for thirty years, was having serious business troubles. At the same time his youngest daughter had been thrown off the back of a motorbike and badly injured, particularly facially. He needed advice and help, and she needed the best plastic surgery which he couldn't afford at that time. I had to spend Christmas and New Year with them.'

'I wondered where you were, and if you were thinking of me.'

'All the time. But missing you, and wanting to see you each time I was passing through London, didn't alter my need for a wife who cared only for me and nothing else.'

'But darling, you can't *not* know how attractive you are as a man, regardless of *Selene* and everything. Never tell me that I'm the first tourist to succumb to your charm when you were on one of your retreats.'

'I rarely encountered any tourists. All the women I've known have known me as John Roxburgh,' he told her. 'As some gossip is sure to tell you about it, perhaps you should know that, then I was in my early twenties, I was engaged to a girl who turned out to be in love with someone else. That only came to light by chance. She'd been pressured into our engagement by an ambitious mother, but nevertheless she did a brilliant job of hiding her real feelings and simulating false ones. I thought she was as crazy about me as I was, then, about her. It taught me that few women can't play a part, and many of them are acting all the time.'

'But not all of us.'

'Not all of you,' he agreed. 'Why didn't you tell me you felt unable to leave your grandfather? You used every other argument but that one.'

'Perhaps because it was my strongest argument, and I knew in my heart that it would never do for a man such as Dion Stefanides to come to England and play second fiddle to his wife. When I met Roderick, he said that in their particular conflict of interests, it would be Lucia who would give in eventually because that was the way women wanted it.'

'You must meet Lucia later this year. I think you would like each other. Meanwhile, for some time to come, I want you to myself, Mrs Roxburgh.'

His arms closed round her. An instant later it was she who was lying on her back with Dion leaning over her.

She put a hand up to his face, tracing the tilt of his cheekbone and the hard male line of his jaw.

She was only half teasing as she murmured, 'Whatever you say . . . my lord and master.'

Harlequin Plus

LOVE SUPERSTITIONS

Many of us who are single may sometimes wish for a crystal ball to tell our futures—especially in the area of love. Failing that, there are a number of little incidents that are said to prophesy what the future holds. We are not suggesting that these things have any real basis in fact, of course, but just for fun you might like to know of a few. If you find that one comes true for you, we'd be delighted to hear about it!

If a cat washes its face in front of a group of people, then looks at you, you will be the first in the group to marry.

You know that the man you love will propose if a white pigeon lands on your doorstep.

If a white speck appears on your little fingernail, then be prepared for a new love.

You will be married before the year is out if you *accidentally* step on a cat's tail.

If you want to sneeze but cannot, it means that someone loves you but is afraid to confess his feelings.

If your forefinger and little finger can touch over the back of your middle finger, you may marry anyone you choose.